BETHLEHEM ROAD

BETHLEHEM ROAD

stories of
immigration
and exile

JUDY LEV

SHE WRITES PRESS

Published in 2025 by
She Writes Press, an imprint of The Stable Book Group

32 Court Street, Suite 2109
Brooklyn, NY 11201
https://shewritespress.com

ISBN: 978-1-64742-998-0
eISBN: 978-1-64742-999-7
Library of Congress Control Number: 2025908961

Interior design by Stacey Aaronson

All drawings for "Meet Your Neighbor" are by illustrator Cookie Moon.
Web: https://www.cookie-moon.com
Instagram: @thecookiemoon.
Email: cookielaimon@gmail.com

Printed in the United States of America

BETHLEHEM
ROAD

TABLE OF CONTENTS

FAMILY LIFE

. . . and you shall be comforted in Jerusalem.
Isaiah 66:13

DISPERSION

...for the days of your slaughter and dispersions have come...

Jeremiah 25:34

PREFACE

Come, and let us go up to the mountain of the Lord.

Isaiah 2:3

I went up to Jerusalem in 1967 and stayed thirty-eight years.

Three months before I left the city, I began the first story in this collection.

After finishing one story, I started another. The stories eased the pain of leaving the Holy City of Jerusalem. The more I wrote and rewrote, the clearer it became that writing these stories would enable me to let go of Jerusalem, but also, paradoxically, to hold on to Bethlehem Road, the street where I raised my children.

Throughout the writing, I fell in love with Baka all over again, the neighborhood in which Bethlehem Road serves as the main artery. This was the setting where I lived as an American immigrant from 1967 to 2005. I appreciated how fortunate I was to have lived and raised three children in such a diverse, vibrant urban neighborhood. Slowly, Bethlehem Road took on mythic proportions. The street became a microcosm of Israel's immigrant society.

As I aged and studied, I understood that Isaiah's invitation—*Come, and let us go up to the mountain of the Lord*—was actually a vision of the heavenly Jerusalem. That other Jerusalem, the heavenly one, is an idyllic utopian place that exists in the collective imagination. There, not in Baka, will we walk in God's paths of justice, righteousness, humility, and compassion; there, where waters will flow uphill and peace will reign, will we hear the Word of the Lord. The stories in *Bethlehem Road* reflect this journey, from idealistic innocence to the everyday experience of Israeli life, from the dream to the mundane.

One day, after years of writing, the stories became more important to me than the street, the characters more real than the people I knew on Bethlehem Road. That was the day I realized I could survive without Baka because I had stories. I had traveled the circular route from exile to immigration and back to exile, both a physical and a psychic journey. In fact, maybe the whole experience of living in Israel has been one long exercise in immigration and exile.

Now it is time to share these stories with you, who have never seen Jerusalem; and you, who have visited and yearn to return; you, who have seen and can't understand what's the big deal; and you, who still live in Baka and either sing its praises or moan its "progress."

Come, let us go up. We will begin near the Sonol Gas Station across the street from Hell Valley (Gehennom) and Mount Zion. We will listen to the voices behind the stone fences, uncover the dreams behind iron gates, feel the pulse that beats in the hearts of those who live on the road between God's mountain and manger. *Yallah*, let's go. Enough preambling.

IMMIGRATION

The Lord builds Jerusalem;
he gathers together the outcasts of Israel.

PSALMS 147:2

INGATHERING OF
AN EXILE

Dear Son,

Your mom and I understand your pull toward Christchurch.
We love reading about the parks and your treks in NZ.
While your decision to spend another year there breaks our
hearts, we would never tell you what to do, given our own
life choices. Meanwhile, please keep writing us. Know that I
love you and will always love you. No matter what. Thanks
for asking about my decision. Here's the short version.
Abba

A reporter from *The Trib* called me looking for stories. He wanted to know how Chicagoans were experiencing the tension before and during the '67 war. I showed up at the King David Hotel on June 7 at 8:00 a.m., mainly for a decent bathroom and a free breakfast. The place was empty, save for those reporters who came expecting to witness Israel's destruction. Grandma kept the article. It's in one of the albums in the attic, twenty-one-year-old me gazing at the walls of the Old City from the veranda of the King David.

After the interview, I walked back up Bethlehem Road toward the *ulpan* on Rehov Gad. That's where I stayed during the war, alone. All the other students went to volunteer at Kibbutz Saad or Ruhama near Gaza. I remember these names because they didn't stop talking about their "war" experiences when they returned at the end of June. Most of them gathered eggs in a chicken coop or cleaned floors in the nurseries.

So on my way back to the *ulpan*, I hear a frightening boom. All around me the sky is a powdery blue, *t'chelet*, but ahead of me on Bethlehem Road, a black cloud. In the shape of a *samech*. I figure the Jordanians hit the gas station just beyond the tracks. My stomach sinks to my socks. I start to shake. I remember exactly where I was standing—next to the stone wall adjacent to the railroad tracks. The man in charge of operating the barrier motions me to come to his shack, but I can't. I'm shaking and frozen at the same time. Parts of me move, but I'm immobile. Two days earlier a shell fell near the Allenby Camp on Hebron Road. Another fell in Makor Haim when I was eating lunch. Each time I panicked. I probably should have gone to a kibbutz just to get out of the line of fire, but who knew? Now my whole body—arms, legs, head—starts shaking uncontrollably. This scares me more than the explosion, so I turn around and force my legs to run. At the first open gate on Bethlehem Road I stop. Thank God I can at least read a Hebrew sign after four months of *ulpan*. It says MINISTRY OF HEALTH. The smaller print I can't read.

The gate leads to a compound of one-story asbestos buildings in the shape of a *chet*. A lone pine stands in the center, bordered on all sides by a garden of geraniums, rosemary, and lavender. I force myself to take a deep breath. My legs relax, but my hands and head are still shaking.

The path leads to a closed door. The sign says KA-BA-LA, reception, just like the sign at the *ulpan*. Below that KA-BA-LA sign, during the first week of *ulpan*, I met your mom. How many times have you heard that story?

I open the door and walk into this office, telling my head and hands to relax.

"I saw an explosion," I tell the woman behind the desk. She's talking on the phone. A beautiful Yemenite. "I mean it's still happening," I say. "It's inside me." I touch my stomach.

She puts down the receiver and looks at me. "Have a drink," she says, and points toward the sink in the hallway. I go to the sink. There are no cups, so I splash water on my face, but the water goes all over the place because my hands are still shaking. Then I go pee in the bathroom. When I come back to her—long black curls, teeth white as the bathroom tiles—she tells me to fill out a form. I have no idea where I am, but I know I don't want to go back to Bethlehem Road, so I write my name and follow the arrow to this small waiting room with no door. The walls are like cardboard. There's an oil painting of Mount Zion at sunset when the city turns pink and gold. On the opposite wall are black-and-white photos of Levi Eshkol, the prime minister, and Zalman Shazar, the president.

"I heard an explosion," I say, standing in the doorway. "Did you hear it too?"

There's a low table in the middle of the room with a glass top strewn with newspapers and magazines. Moshe Dayan's face stares at me from a front page. Funny, what details you remember on days that change your life. Four people are sitting around the table on folding chairs, their heads bent. They look up at me as if I'm crazy. "Did you hear it?" I say. This one woman with a crochet hook in hand gives me a look as if I am unworthy of her time. Opposite me a disheveled ultra-Orthodox man rocks back and forth in his chair, sucking his *peyot*. Strangest thing I ever saw. This guy on my right, who looks familiar, is sitting with his arm around an empty chair. There's something weird about him. His eyes are two different colors—one brown, the other blue. He doesn't offer me the empty chair, so I ask if I can sit down.

"Did you hear the explosion?" I ask him in English.

"Ovadia," he says, "Ovadia Levi," and puts his hand in my face. That's how I first met the falafel man. I shake his hand, oily with a layer of grime. "You're shaking," he tells me. "No, I didn't hear anything special today. But I've been hearing explosions for twenty years."

He's almost sitting on top of me and starts telling me about how he lost his eye in the Battle for Jerusalem in the War of Independence and his left eye is glass and I'm worried he's going to take it out to show me. He's looking into my eyes as if I'm a cauldron of hot oil. I feel uncomfortable sitting so close to him, so I slide the chair toward the doorway, but he just keeps talking about the battle in '48, how the mine exploded against the wall of the Hurva Synagogue and how shrapnel landed in his leg and in his head, how the pain has never left him, how he manages with one eye despite the constant headaches.

"The Jewish people lose the Old City," he says, "and I lose an eye."

This was my first meaningful sentence in Hebrew: *Ha'am ha'yehudi ma'abed et Ir Ha'atika v'ani ma'abed ayin.* Then he says he's lucky because after the War of Independence, the state put him and his wife into an apartment on Bethlehem Road with some other family, and he tells me how Baka was Arab, but after the war the state filled it with Jews from all over, and how the state gave him a falafel shack as compensation for the eye and how he raised three kids on falafel balls, tahini, and pickles. The pickles his wife made.

By the end of Ovadia's story, my hands are shaking less.

Some of us from the *ulpan* hung out at Ovadia's falafel stand on Saturday nights, but I never knew the owner was a hero.

"You've heard of Trumpeldor?" he asks me.

"*Tov-la-mut*," I begin, but I can't remember the end of Trumpeldor's famous line, uttered while dying.

". . . *ba'ad-artzenu*," Ovadia says. "I figure if it's good to die for our country, it's no big deal to lose an eye for our country." Then he takes out a small white paper envelope from his shirt pocket and I'm sure he's going to take out his eye and put it in the envelope and I can't decide whether to watch or not watch. During my confusion, he pours out some pink and yellow pills into his hand.

"And here we are fighting again," he says, slowly, sadness in his voice. "Who knew I'd hear explosions every day? These help," he adds, pointing to the pills with his chin.

The receptionist comes in and tells Ovadia that Dr. Yarus can see him now. Ovadia closes the pills in his hand and stands up. He bends down to whisper in my ear. "I lost one eye. Now they think I'm losing my mind." He pats my shoulder. "Don't worry, young man. We'll win this war. Then all the American Jews like you will come home." His breath smells like garlic.

As soon as he leaves the waiting room, the woman sitting opposite says, "You want explosions? I'll tell you a story. You know '56? You know Bir Gafgafa?"

She's crocheting a kippa, and her daughter next to her—maybe eleven or twelve—leans into her, as if they are physically attached. Every few stitches, the mother tries pushing her away, but the daughter leans right back.

Bir Gafgafa? Never heard of the place. I just know the black cloud of smoke above the gas station on Bethlehem Road. My head is shaking and I can't figure out why nobody else in the room seems disturbed by the explosion down the street. It was loud. How could they have missed it? If I'd had a cell phone in those days, I would have called the reporter from *The Trib* right then and there and told him, but who had phones? It took a year just to get a regular old-fashioned rotary dial phone—you know, the kind you saw in the Field Museum.

"1956," she repeats, "when Egypt tried to take control of the canal from the big shots."

She doesn't seem to care if I understand or not.

"So my husband, her father," she says, pushing her daughter, "gets called up. They give him and some other guy from Ness Ziona a heavy load of munitions to drive from Tzrifin to Bir Gafgafa. You know where is Tzrifin?"

She doesn't wait for my response.

"So I'm home with two little girls and pregnant with this one," she says, poking the crochet hook into her daughter's arm. "This is November 3, 1956. So on November 5, two soldiers come to my house, my shitty little apartment in the *shikun* at the end of Bethlehem Road. You know this neighborhood? You fancy American. You probably don't know what it means when two soldiers knock on your door."

While she continues her tirade, the black cloud triggers little explosions in my gut.

"This is how the army tells you your husband is dead—they send two *pishers*, younger than you even, to say, 'You are now a widow and the Ministry of Defense will take care of you.'" She puts her hand on her daughter. "They didn't know she was inside. I start screaming, so the whole *shikun* comes into my apartment because they hear me and everyone is afraid I lose my baby. I swear on four Bibles, at that moment I wanted to lose her. Every day of the shiva I sit on the floor and tear out my hair and scratch my cheeks till they bleed. All day I scream at God.

"I already lost my husband and my mind, but this God, he has more surprises for me. On the fifth day of the shiva two more soldiers come to my door. 'Who else could die?' I ask them and they tell me, 'It was a mistake. Yes, there was an explosion, yes, somebody died, but not your husband. It was the one from Ness Ziona. Your husband is wounded in Be'er Sheva,' they tell me. 'We're sorry,' they say. I don't know anymore what to say, so I collapse."

Fortunately, the receptionist comes in again and tells this woman that Anita is ready to see her and her daughter. The woman yells at her daughter to get up.

I feel sorry for these people and wonder how the Ministry of Health can help them. I can tell the ultra-Orthodox man sitting in that waiting room catty-corner from me has heard every word of our conversation, but he doesn't react until the mother and girl leave.

Then he stops sucking his *peyot* and takes out a screwdriver from the inside pocket of his floppy jacket. He puts the metal side of the screwdriver in his mouth.

"Did you hear the explosion?" I ask.

He holds the screwdriver steady in his mouth and looks down at the table while he produces scraps of story. "April 27, 1939. Father and me. Bethlehem Road. Three-thirty to my uncle. Talpiot. Father and me. Mortar. Father dead."

The telling sounds like a mantra. As he repeats it a second time, he turns the screwdriver in his mouth and rocks back and forth as if praying.

Fortunately, the beautiful Yemenite receptionist comes in again and tells him Nechama is ready to see him. I didn't know then that *nechama* means "compassion."

The man stops rocking and puts the screwdriver back into his jacket. He walks by me gazing at the floor, bent like a cane. Then the Yemenite turns to me and says the intake worker can see me.

"What intake worker?" I say. "I came ..."

"You have a problem, no? Gila ..."

I'm not sure what I have or why I came. Nothing is shaking anymore, but I heard and saw an explosion. I was scared. Now I am confused and more scared, after all these stories and their tellers who didn't hear or see any explosion that day. Who was crazy here? Grandma and Grandpa were waiting for me to return to Chicago. They were furious I didn't leave in May, before the war. Every week Grandma called the *ulpan* and threatened to die if I didn't come home.

"I heard an explosion," I say.

"Gila is in Room Three," she says, pointing to the room with the green door.

What a name, Gila—"happiness." Good thing I didn't know that then. I walk to Room Three. The lone pine in the center of the garden threatens. I crawl deeper into my skin. If I'd had a screwdriver, I would have tightened my heart.

Inside the room Gila sits behind a wooden desk, all smiles and black-framed glasses. She has a birthmark like a *yud* under her lip.

"What happened?" she asks, as I tremble on the folding chair opposite her.

"I was at the King David talking to *The Trib* and walking back to the *ulpan* and right after the railroad tracks I saw an explosion. I mean I was standing *before* the railroad tracks and I saw and heard the explosion. Over the gas station. An enormous black cloud. A terrible boom. Like nothing before. As if something hit me deep. Inside. My whole body shook, but no blood.

"I was lucky and avoided the draft to Vietnam, but now I'm in a war zone and this bomb scared me to death and my family wants me home. I love Jerusalem. Part of me wants to stay when the *ulpan* ends, but another part wants to go to law school. I have a full scholarship at Michigan, but I want to teach Hitler a lesson. That's more important, don't you think?"

I can't believe my own words and I hope Gila understands. She gives me a coy smile and asks, "Why don't you just decide to stay?"

She doesn't know my parents. It would kill them if I stay, I tell her. She doesn't understand what it means to receive a full scholarship to the University of Michigan Law School. I tell her I want to feel connected to Israel, so I practice all the words to "Jerusalem of Gold." I hum and sing.

She nods her head yes and says, "Um," so I assume she understands. Her eyes accept me. Then I begin to cry. Yes. Me, your father, who never cries.

She asks again why I don't stay, but I *am* staying, I tell myself. I'm here, aren't I?

"I want to join the Israeli army." Here I am dodging the draft all during Northwestern and now I want to join the army? I see and hear an explosion, my whole body shakes, and I want to be a soldier? I don't know what I want. "Am I crazy?"

"Everyone here has a war story," she says, checking my name on the form. "This is yours, Yonatan."

"John," I say.

"Yonatan," she says. "Whenever you want to talk to me again, you know where to find me."

Gila gives me a white envelope with four pills that are available at any druggist without a prescription and tells me to leave my details in Hebrew with the receptionist.

I don't know if I'm insulted or glad.

She stands up and says, "Shalom, Yonatan."

Of course. Beneath the John, there was always this Yonatan. The next day I would go to the Ministry of the Interior and change my name. I wanted a name that reverberated with at least two thousand years of history.

I thanked Gila, left the room, and walked back to the receptionist. On a blank page I wrote my name and address in Hebrew: "Yonatan Silver. Ulpan Etzion." On the path leading to the gate, the lone pine called again. This time the trunk looked like a *vav*.

Back on the sidewalk, I gazed toward the train tracks. There were a few cars on Bethlehem Road. The sky was a safe *t'chelet*. All traces of the black cloud had vanished. As I approached the tracks to cross over, the old guard in the little shed came out to lower the barrier. He shouted at me, "Looks like it's over, son. We have the Old City."

At the gas station there were no signs of fire or smoke, just two attendants laughing and hitting each other on the back. I walked past the old-age home for Holocaust survivors, past the vegetable vendor arranging his cucumbers like a pyramid, past the old shoemaker pounding a sole. I stopped to buy gum at Doda Rosa's candy shack. Mainly I wanted her warm smile. Beyond Rehov Reuven the dry cleaner was spreading a Persian rug on the sidewalk to dry and the butcher was taking in freshly slaughtered chickens from a plastic crate on the curb and putting them, two by two, in his freezer. Across the street, a man from the first floor wearing pajamas was shouting from his porch to the shopkeeper below to move his vegetables off the communal sidewalk. At Ovadia's falafel shack, cab drivers leaned against the iron railing separating the sidewalk from the street, munching their overflowing pitas while tahini rolled down their chins. Were they arguing about the war or celebrating? The guy who sold building supplies across the street stood talking to a pregnant mother holding the hands of two little kids. He pulled out two lollipops from his pocket. Moshe, who owned the corner newsstand, was yelling at someone in a car to bring more newspapers. When I walked into Menachem's bakery on the corner of Bethlehem Road and Yehuda, he threw his arms around my neck and, smelling like cinnamon, kissed my cheeks.

"We won the war," he says. "We won the war, John. Now all you Americans can come home. Tell everyone you know. We won the war."

I'll never forget his excitement, relief, and certainty. It was as if a 2,000-year-old man from the spice trail was giving me a kiss. I had only bought *challot* from him on Friday mornings and here he was handing me a cheese bun straight from the oven and telling me to tell American Jews to start packing.

"Peace! Now we'll have peace," he said over and over . "Peace! Peace!"

"Amen," I said and, "Thank you," and I gave him another hug for feeding me. I told him we'd have to see about all those American Jews, thinking about my parents and grandparents, who expected me home by mid-August, before the academic year began in Ann Arbor.

I walked down Rehov Yehuda to Ulpan Etzion on Gad. All the way I kept thinking of the stories those people told me in the waiting room, about their explosions and my own. I thought about the people on Bethlehem Road. They were like so many actors on a stage, playing their parts every day. I was an observer, walking by, applauding this, struck by that.

As I approached the *ulpan*, I looked down at my hands. No shaking. They smelled like sweet cheese. The idea crystalized. Everyone saw it but me, maybe because I was only twenty-one or maybe because of the tensions of the war, I don't know. At that moment I wanted to come home, to Israel. I wanted to be a player, an actor on the stage, to take part in the miracle, not just watch from the sidelines.

I knew Jerusalem, not Chicago, would be home. I knew my parents and my grandparents would be devastated, but my gut told me I wanted to stay in Israel. I wanted to join the victims struggling to be heroes. I wanted to build a new life in an old language. I wanted to forfeit the expected trajectory and to dive into the unknown.

The pines in the yard adjacent to the *ulpan* beckoned. They stood tall as willing soldiers. I sat down on one of the benches, my legs now shaking for another reason. Looking up, I saw the tips of the pines moving toward each other gracefully, forming all the letters of the Hebrew alphabet. Looking down onto my hands I saw *gimmels*, *vavs*, *mems*, *heys*, the letters engraved in my skin.

Inside the *ulpan*, from a pay phone I called the reporter from *The Trib* at the King David. I told him what happened after I left the hotel. "My own little victory," I said. "Please change my story. And use 'Yonatan.' I'm staying in Israel."

He did not sound surprised.

Doda Rosa, Candy Shack

The children like these tiny dot candies, the pink
and yellow ones on the strip of white paper. I
don't know why. Whenever any of those poor children from Beit Joseph across the street walk by
with their counselor, I call them in and give each
child a few dots. It's no big deal for me, maybe
two agorot for eight dots of colored sugar on a
piece of cheap paper.

A little candy can make a big difference, you
know, even one scrap from a neighbor. Some days in
the camps I drew candy in the dirt and on the floor
with a stick. And cakes and cookies and other
things I remembered from home. Believe it or not,
that helped me survive. This sweet shack is a
blessing. I have work. I earn a few lirot. If I
could, I would give away all the candy for free. We
could get by with one chicken a week. I like to
give, especially to those unfortunate children.
Once, in the camps, someone gave me a half-sucked
scrap of candy and that portion kept me alive. Even
though it was sour. I've treasured the memory, the
taste and that kindness during the war, for thirty
years, ever since I left that place.

Sadly, my son wasn't as lucky.

SIMON, THE TALE OF
AN ASPIRING JEW

S imon Bloomberg yearned to bear the yoke of a God-fearing Jew. He rented a room from an Iraqi woman in a large house on Rehov Shimon across from Ahavat Yisrael synagogue, two houses off Bethlehem Road. Three times a day he followed nine newly repentant men to Ahavat Yisrael. Three times a day he tried to follow their words during prayer. It did not bother him that the nine men chatted in French and Spanish during prayers, but it did bother him that the Hebrew prayers were as foreign to him as the Aramaic Talmud, which he tried to master at night with his *Idiot's Guide to Talmud, Part I.*

The rabbi at Ahavat Yisrael, HaRav Abermesh, enlisted Simon into his Army of the Faithful. In this select group, Simon met other young, single men in their twenties like himself, searching for God and struggling to control their Evil Inclination. HaRav Abermesh took a special liking to Simon because of his devotion, expressed mainly in the length of the ritual fringes he wore over his alligator polo shirts. Simon was proof that God works in mysterious ways, claimed HaRav Abermesh, and that the Messiah was near. "Is it not written in the Holy Book," he asked his soldiers in the Army of the Faithful, "that when the most depraved men from the most depraved countries return to the Lord, the Messiah's footsteps are heard?"

Neither Simon nor anyone else in the group knew enough Bible to answer the rabbi's question. Nonetheless, Simon enjoyed imagining the Messiah resting on an ancient rock inside the Dung Gate, polishing his North Face hiking boots while his bare feet stretched toward the Western Wall, its Herodian stones damp from two thousand years of Jewish tears. Abermesh was an inspiration.

Before meeting the rabbi, Simon had felt torn. But now that he understood that his suffering had been caused not by his parents' divorce when he was seven, nor by his dyslexia, diagnosed at twelve, nor even by his allergies to wheat and milk, diagnosed at sixteen, but, rather, by the Evil Inclination, he could relax. Simon stopped asking questions, returned to white bread and milkshakes, and bought a huge wooden *mezuzah* to hang on the doorframe of his room. Moreover, he convinced Bilha, his Iraqi landlady, to have her mezuzah checked. Sure enough, all the *alephs* were fading. He bought her a new scroll.

The Evil Inclination, Simon learned, was a tricky enemy, always ready to pounce. When memories from Athens, Ohio, and Kibbutz Gal-On distracted Simon from his *Idiot's Guide to Talmud, Part I* by tempting him to turn on and bed buxom freshmen or Danish volunteers, he knew the Evil Inclination was afoot. On such occasions, Simon took his book, walked over to Falafel Ovadia, and ordered a *laffa*. The small falafel balls wrapped in the large, warm pita reminded Simon that, like them, he was wrapped in God's loving-kindness. Falafel suppressed his Evil Inclination, at least temporarily.

On one such day in Shvat, after a heavy rain had left the air luminous as crystal, Simon spotted an American woman with his mother's complexion sitting at a white plastic table. She was talking to a younger woman.

"After twelve years of carobs and water, the Bat Kol sent them back into the cave," the elder explained in a teacher's voice, "because they destroyed everything they looked at. Their studiousness proved dangerous to G-d's world."

This woman's voice enticed Simon to stand next to their table, falafel and all.

"I'm Simon Bloomberg," he interrupted. "Do you mind if I listen?"

"Bracha Finkelstein," said the older woman. Her eyes were like deep wells. When she looked at him, Simon felt himself falling in. Surely, God had placed this woman at Ovadia's falafel shack to help him change his life. Bracha lowered her eyes, a gesture that made Simon's heart flutter. Her hair was black and comely as the tents of Kedar.

Bracha continued to explicate the story of Rabbi Shimon bar Yochai. "So they sat in the cave another year, buried in sand to their heads, naked."

"Why naked?" the younger woman asked.

Simon didn't care. He just wanted to hear Bracha's voice. It tickled all the steps of his spine.

"They didn't want their clothes to wear out. They only got dressed for daily prayers," Bracha said.

"What did they do all day?"

The younger woman struck Simon as a nudnik, but when he heard Bracha's reply, all negative thoughts vanished.

"They studied."

Bracha's intonation made Simon understand that studying was, indeed, next to godliness.

The sky that revealed unimaginable light in Shvat continued to shine for Simon through Adar. After three weeks of *laffas*, *gemmorahs*, and a raucous Purim party at the Efrata Seminary, where Bracha was studying to become a kindergarten teacher, Simon knew. Bracha was everything he had imagined when he was still a depraved kibbutz volunteer. She had studied Talmud at Stern College, one of those eastern women's schools that Simon had never heard of until he left the Midwest for Israel. She owned an apartment in the Jewish Quarter of the Old City of Jerusalem. "I must live close to the Holy Presence," she told Simon, when he asked why there and not Baka. She was the best student at the Efrata Seminary and, even though she had another profession, accounting, she was now preparing to fulfill her deepest longing— to guide little children into the arms of a loving God. Simon knew Bracha would want to support a husband, one who would study Talmud all day.

The fact that Bracha was eighteen years older than Simon, twice divorced, and the mother of two children in Brooklyn convinced him that she had struggled with the Evil Inclination herself, and won. Her trials had brought her firmly to the feet of the Holy One, Blessed be He.

Simon knew he could master the *Idiot's Guide to Talmud, Part I*—maybe even *Part II*—with Bracha's help. Her teeth were clean sheep coming up from the river. Were her cheeks not like pomegranates?

After Purim, Simon met Bracha regularly at Ovadia's and

listened to her explicate the Talmud. On the Sunday after Shabbat HaGadol, he proposed.

Why Bracha agreed to marry Simon was anyone's guess. Ovadia ascribed it to the magic ingredients he put in his falafel balls and promised to cater the wedding.

"God has been working on this match since the parting of the Red Sea," said HaRav Abermesh.

Bilha, the Iraqi landlady, who loved listening to soccer matches on the radio on Shabbat afternoons while eating Kurdish meatballs, told Simon he was making a tragic mistake. She forbade him to bring Bracha to her house.

"Not before the wedding and not after. *Yesh lanu hozeh*," she said, as if speaking to a rooster. "We have a contract."

Simon ascribed Bilha's ill will to the Evil Inclination.

On a glorious day during the Counting of the Omer, Simon and Bracha rode the number 6 bus to Zion Square on Jaffa Road, walked up Street of the Lily, and leapt, like two mountain goats prancing on the cragged hills of Ein Gedi, into the Jerusalem Rabbinate. Simon negotiated with two American smart alecks hanging around the men's room on the third floor to act as witnesses. The meeting with the officiating rabbi went smoothly, until the rabbi, a white beard touching his belt, turned to Simon and asked, "Are you a Yid? Do you have proof?"

"What's a Yid?" Simon whispered to Bracha.

"A Jew," she whispered back.

Simon began to unzip his fly. Bracha cringed.

"No, no. Not that, you dummy," shouted the rabbi. "I need written proof, a document, some text. These witnesses you Americans bring, we know this trick. A text I need."

Simon felt embarrassed for acting like a fool in front of

Bracha. "It was the Evil Inclination," he explained, as they walked back to Jaffa Road, "trying to undermine my desire."

Bracha quoted a line from Isaiah about forgiveness. "Just as the Holy One, Blessed be He, forgave His chosen people for their sins, so I, too, forgive your stupidity."

Simon wanted to hug his bride-to-be right there, across the street from the Ministry of the Interior, but remembered he was not allowed to touch her until the night of the wedding. Instead, he played with his ritual fringes and sucked his upper lip.

When he returned to his rented room, Simon wrote his mother a letter asking for a document that would attest to his Jewishness. *I know this may sound strange, Mom, but these are the ways in my new chosen land. I am sure you will grow to love Bracha, even though she used to root for the Dodgers. BTW, have you spoken to Dad lately?*

He ran to the post office, mailed the letter express, and waited.

A week later, Bracha and Simon sat at Ovadia's. Bracha was explaining to Simon what his namesake, Rabban Shimon ben Gamliel the Elder, had been doing during the Great Revolt of 66–70 CE and how that affected the lineage of the presidents of the Sanhedrin, when she suddenly stopped in mid-sentence.

"What if the document isn't acceptable?" she blurted. "Your mother doesn't observe *nida*, does she?"

The word sounded familiar to Simon. Was it a Shabbat practice or a stance with a 9 iron? Simon felt the Evil Inclination dredging his former life, mixing it up with his revised, new self like some sadistic juggler, some nasty clown.

"Bracha," he said, "I am so ashamed of my ignorance."

"Why, my sweet?" She wiped tahini from her chin.

"I am such a dumb Jew. I am so far from being God-fearing. I've never even heard of Lag B'Omer." He straightened his kippa on his head. "I need time by myself, Bracha." The words surprised him as much as they did his fiancée.

"Are you afraid of commitment?" she asked.

"No, not that. Didn't Moses go into the wilderness? Didn't Jesus stay in a cave for forty days before his transformation?"

No sooner had Simon finished his question than he became squeamish for invoking that no-goodnik, who had brought so much suffering to the Jewish people.

Bracha released her tightened lips and relaxed her nostrils. "Go, my sweet," she sang. "I trust the Lord will watch over you. I will be here when you return, just as Rachel waited for her Akiva. But, remember, always cover your head."

During the first week of their meetings at Ovadia's, Simon had donned a small white kippa circled with brown embroidery that echoed the crenelated walls of the Old City. As his love for Bracha grew, so did his head covering. Now he wore a colorful Bukharian kippa that covered the lobes of his elephant ears. With each incremental growth in his kippa, Simon felt closer to the Holy One, Blessed be He.

On the bus to Tel Aviv, Simon thought about Shimon bar Yochai. He loved listening to Bracha tell the story of how this Shimon had buried himself in sand up to his head and studied Torah while he hid in a cave from the Romans. Simon Bloomberg imagined burying himself on the beach at Nahariya and reading his *Idiot's Guide to Talmud, Part I*. Surely that would make a good impression on Bracha. No matter what the rabbi on Street of the Lily decided, Simon's taking the words of the Talmud seriously, choosing them as a map for his new life, would prove that he was a true—What was the word?—*Yid*. He would study the chapter on *nida*.

When he arrived in Tel Aviv, Simon went to the information booth and learned that the next bus to Nahariya would leave in two hours. He wandered the filthy streets near the central bus station and bought a *laffa* at a greasy stand endorsed by the chief Sephardic rabbi of Tel Aviv. While eating, he thought about his new life in Jerusalem—HaRav Abermesh and his militant faithful; his landlady Bilha, who still refused to light Shabbat candles despite his nudging; Torah-observant Ovadia and the secular city inspectors who, like Roman soldiers, harassed him to move his plastic tables from the sidewalk; *Idiot's Guide to Talmud, Part I*, which he carried faithfully in his backpack like a talisman; and Bracha, her holy fire, the key to his future. It was good to have time on his own to assess his progress and deepen his commitment to becoming a God-fearing Jew.

But then he wondered if this little trip up north was a visitation from the Evil Inclination. How could one tell?

At 1:00 p.m. he boarded the bus. It arrived, not in Nahariya, but in Nazareth. In his former, secular life he would have cursed the driver and the driver's mother. Now God was leading and Simon followed. Does not the Holy One, Blessed be He, hear our thoughts and prayers in Nazareth, Nahariya, and Nahalal? What difference does place make? The main thing is *kavanna*, intention.

Simon wandered around Nazareth, weighed doing the cave thing in the basement of the Church of the Annunciation and vetoed it, assuming Bracha would not look favorably on a Yid studying Talmud in a church.

Quickly, he returned to the bus station and caught the last bus to Haifa. In Haifa, he raced to the train station and jumped on the last train to Nahariya. When he arrived, the sea was accepting the setting sun.

26

Where would he sleep the first night of his journey? Simon didn't worry. If he had learned anything from HaRav Abermesh it was that God provides. Therefore, Simon didn't need reservations. He walked to the beach. Nobody was there, save for a family with two naked children, a girl and a boy, who were sitting on the shore. The bronzed children dug into the wet sand with red plastic shovels and filled their plastic pails. When their pails were full, they dumped the sand behind them and made a fortress. Their parents watched from the entrance to their tent.

Simon lay down on the sand several meters behind the family. He enjoyed the twilight wind hovering over his body like the Shekhina. He wanted to press it into his *tzitzit*, but the wind did not cooperate. He removed his sandals and placed them next to his backpack. Sitting up, he buried his toes in the sand. It felt cool, so he pushed his feet deeper until the sand covered his calves and then his knees. As he shifted sand onto his thighs, he wondered how bar Yochai had found enough sand in a cave and how he survived on carob for twelve years. At the Purim party, tasting carob ice cream had almost made Simon puke. He would never reach bar Yochai's degree of devotion.

Simon covered his crotch with the pure, white sand and, with his arms flailing behind him, made a small incline for his back. Thus he sat at sunset, covered in sand to his waist, watching the waves lap the shore with a force that only the Holy One understood. He reached into his backpack for *Idiot's Guide to Talmud, Part I* and in the index looked up "*nida*."

The two naked children watched, pointed, and laughed. With his left hand, Simon motioned them to approach. He would tell the children the story of bar Yochai, encouraging them to study. If little Jewish boys studied Torah and covered their heads, if little

Jewish girls lit Shabbat candles, the Messiah would come. Was the Messiah not at the Dung Gate right now, polishing his hiking boots? Maybe he would arrive in Baka before his mother's letter.

The children looked at each other. For a moment they reminded Simon of a midrash Bracha had told him. After the destruction of the Holy Temple, there were two beautiful children who were enslaved to Romans. The Romans wanted them to marry each other in order to produce more beautiful children for the enjoyment of the depraved conquerors. Rather than marry, the children talked all night and cried, because they had discovered they were brother and sister. By the morning, they were dead.

Simon thought about Romans and their lust for child sex. He banished a lewd image from his brain, sent, no doubt, by his Evil Inclination.

The children on the beach stood up, threw their sand buckets and shovels next to their parents, who were cuddling under the tent awning, and ran to Simon. They looked no more than eight or nine, like the children in the midrash. Their golden skin made their teeth glow like meringue. When the little girl tickled Simon's left shoulder, he was taken aback. He reached out to swat her.

"Don't hit my sister, or we'll bury you," the little boy said, grabbing Simon's Bukharian kippa. He threw it to the wind.

"You little mother . . ." As Simon began to move his legs in an effort to release the weight of the sand, the boy jumped on his back and pulled him down. His sister straddled Simon's chest. Who were these kids? Messengers from the devil? Was this a test?

"Let's bury him," the girl said to her brother.

Simon wriggled to get free, but the two little monsters had him pinned to the sand and were heaping sand on his chest. Surely the parents could hear and would come immediately. When Simon began to speak, the boy threw sand into his mouth. Simon spit and then kept his mouth shut, cursing them silently. Pieces of snot. May the Angel of Death visit them before their bar and bat mitzvah.

He felt guilty cursing little children, even silently, and told the Evil Inclination to take a swim. When the little girl flung *Idiot's Guide to Talmud, Part I* to the wind, his guilt vanished. He wailed a loud "Shiiit" as the sister sat on his left forearm and buried his hand and his elbow. The brother did the same on the right. Surely the parents would come to see what the ruckus was about, though Simon sensed this was not the first time these urchins had buried a man in the sand. Did the local authorities know about these demons? He would report them as soon as he was free to move.

The brother packed sand around Simon's ears, while the sister covered his neck. Surely, they would stop here. Simon let out a cry aimed at the parents, but nobody came. His cry seemed to egg on the children.

When he felt the girl's hand covering his lips, he forced his mouth open and bit her finger. Then he started to yell, "God, help me."

The brother threw sand at his face.

"Help," Simon cried.

Nobody came to help. Maybe the urchins' parents were deaf. Maybe the Angel of Death had taken them on a Mediterranean cruise. God, too, did not respond.

"That's enough, Joshua," the girl said to her brother. "Remember what happened last time." She stood up. "Let's go back to the fort." She ran toward the water and her brother stood up, but before he followed, he dropped a handful of sand on Simon's face.

It was almost dark now. Simon couldn't believe that such evil existed in the world. His own Evil Inclination was one thing. True, it meandered between lewd images, nasty ideas, and evil thoughts, but nothing like this. He was an angel compared to these devils.

He closed his eyes, but it was no use. The grains felt like cut glass on his eyeballs. Then he remembered a biblical verse, something about Israel being a land that devours its inhabitants. He would ask Bracha for the exact quote.

The parents stood up and walked to their children on the shoreline. Simon heard them yell to get dressed so they could go home and watch the news.

Simon moved his head from side to side to release the sand from his cheeks and lips. With much effort, his left hand broke through the surface. He brushed off the sand around his neck. His breathing felt grainy and constricted and for a second he feared he might die on the shore, the victim of child abuse. God worked in mysterious ways, but this was ridiculous. If Bracha ever heard this story, she would think him a true idiot and cancel the marriage. He debated with himself whether or not to confront the parents and let them know their children were devils. In the end, he chose the easy way, which was to say nothing.

That night Simon Bloomberg slept on the beach with sand covering his lower body like a blanket. He dreamed of familiar bars in Athens and of Danes in the vineyards of Gal-On. When he awoke at sunrise, the world of his dreams seemed more attractive than the sand of the Holy Land. How could this be? He missed debauchery. Surely, the Evil Inclination was after his soul, juggling with him, confusing him to the point of passivity. "Whose life is this?" he shouted to the shore. "Who makes my decisions?" he asked the sand. He neither sensed nor heard the Shekhina.

Simon wrestled himself free from the sand and walked into

the water to drown yesterday's nightmare. Seaweed and muck entangled his toes. He howled.

"Lord of the Universe, how much? Till when?"

The answer was not long in coming. After Simon returned to his backpack and sandals, a green jeep rode by with a young, bald driver, spreading the familiar smell of weed.

"No loiterers, fellow. I'm going to have to fine you one hundred *lirot* for sleeping on the beach."

Simon's tongue stuck to the roof of his mouth. Why was this happening? He had not forgotten Jerusalem, not for a moment; well, maybe while sleeping. Awake, he always held Jerusalem above his highest joy. Simon ran barefoot toward the rising sun. Surely the driver would understand, but the driver took out his pistol. Simon heard the shot. The bullet skimmed his head and hit a garbage bin overflowing with yesterday's debris.

Two days later Simon returned to the smell of fried onions in Bilha's house. A changed man, he did not kiss the mezuzah. He saw the nine men go into Ahavat Yisrael in the late afternoon and did not join them. Bilha handed him his mail. He fingered the brown envelope and missed his mother.

That night, he met Bracha at Ovadia's falafel shack. For the first time since they had met, he noticed lines on either side of her nose that led to her upper lip, as if she were a marionette. Where had they been hiding before? An orange hue covered the upper halves of her two front teeth. Was he blind? Was she a chain smoker? She smelled like spoiled corn oil.

"Bracha," he said, shaking his head side to side and stammering, as if he were Moses.

"Yes, my love," said Bracha, looking at the scratches on his arms. "Where is your kippa?"

"Bracha," he said, head still shaking and now closing his eyes.

"Yes, Shimi," she said softly.

Shimi? Who was Shimi? This was the first time he had heard the name.

"Remember when you told me about bar Yochai?" he asked.

"Of course I remember, my love. Do angels have wings?"

What did angels have to do with this? He felt the same frustration he had felt in seventh grade when he couldn't read what the history teacher had written on the board.

"Forget the angels, Bracha. I went to Nahariya to see if I could survive studying for one day in sand."

"Like your namesake?"

"Yes." He opened his eyes and walked over to the counter. "Give me some pickles, please." Ovadia put two wrapped in paper right into the palm of his hand. He returned to his chair and slammed on the table. "I don't believe this joker lived thirteen years in a cave." He was surprised at the ferocity of his words. "I don't believe he lived thirteen *weeks* in a cave."

"What are you saying, Shimi?"

"Don't call me Shimi," he said with an unfamiliar determination. "I'm saying that his mother probably lived down the road and brought him Kurdish meatballs every day, like Thoreau's."

"Who?"

"Either the story is false or this Shimon was a greater man than I will ever be."

"You are young, Shimi."

"Don't say that. I am the age of your son, to be exact, but I have a brain and it tells me—"

"Say no more, my love. I cannot bear this." Bracha picked up her soiled napkin and wiped her eyes.

Simon put the brown envelope on the table. "The letter," he announced, as if delivering a verdict.

"Finally," she said, "the rabbis will be satisfied you are a proper Yid. Open it, my love. But first, buy me a *laffa*."

He bought Bracha a *laffa* smothered with tahini and *zhug*. In the brown envelope were a document and a smaller, violet envelope. He placed the violet envelope on the table and held up the document. At the top in large roman typeface was the name "The Holy Blossom Temple." Under it, in smaller letters, was the address "2849 Gate of Heaven Road, Cincinnati, Ohio, United States of America." He read the text softly: "This is to certify that Simon Peter Hillside, son of Mary and James Hillside, was confirmed on the twentieth of June, 1966, in the main sanctuary of The Holy Blossom Temple, Cincinnati, Ohio."

The document was signed by Rabbi Paul S. Stockley, Assistant Rabbi. In the lower left corner was a yellow print of a haystack and an American flag. The words "Central Conference of American Rabbis" were stamped over the drawing. In the lower right corner was Hebrew writing that Simon couldn't read.

Bracha's lower jaw dropped. Her lips, which had once conjured wine, now conjured vinegar. Simon put the document on the table, gently lifted his mother's stationery, and tore open the seal. Inside was a piece of violet onionskin paper with purple handwriting. He unfolded it and read aloud.

"Dear Si, I hope this document is the one you wanted. It states your name (the one you were christened by, as your father used to joke), our names, and the rabbi's name. I hope the fact that it's only the assistant rabbi isn't a problem. They don't have to know Stockley stayed two years at Holy Blossom before leaving the rabbinate for pro golf, do they? Barbara sounds like a bright girl, but I am worried she is so much older than you and has children. Maybe you should wait. Israel seems to have taken hold of you. Rome wasn't built in a day, remember. Anyway, I look forward to meeting . . . Bonna? Batya? when you come home for Christmas vacation. By the way, what does her name mean? Is it Hebrew?

"Despite your love of Israel and things Jewish, I still hope you will decide to settle down in Ohio and take over Grandpa's trucking business, which is doing well. I'm sure B. could find work at Holy Blossom Sunday School. You could continue your studies of Talmud at HUC. You don't have to live in Israel to study it, right?

"Have you written to your father about your plans? Please tell me what I should say and not say.

"I am buried in golf tournaments this summer and hardly have time to breathe. Having trouble staying out of sand traps.

"Let me know if the rabbi there needs anything else. I'll send whatever other documents he needs, though I repeat, I am not happy with this match. Does he play golf or tennis, the rabbi? I hope you are watching your diet, Si. I love you and send you hugs and kisses. As always, Mom."

The longer Simon Bloomberg stared at his mother's letter, the more her cursive resembled Rashi's, an alphabet from a distant world. He heard his mother's voice behind the written words, but that too sounded foreign. He had left a broken home, strayed, discovered a new world, and now, he realized, he had lost the one home he had ever known and loved, for which there could be no substitute, anywhere, ever.

He slid down the chair onto the sidewalk. As he slid, he crumpled his mother's letter in his hand. With his arms covering his bare head, he moaned, as if an eternal ache had suddenly risen to the surface. He felt homeless in what was supposed to be his homeland.

The Evil Inclination giggled. Simon lashed out his arms in all directions, as if swatting an invisible fly. His moan turned to a cry. "Ahhhhhhh." He lifted himself back onto the chair. Bracha looked at him as if he had gone mad.

"I cannot marry you, Bracha." His voice came from the bottom of his gut with no stuttering.

"Why, my love?"

"Because there is no I behind my I."

Bracha stared, dumbstruck. "No eye behind your eye?"

"No me behind you and me. No me in myself."

"You talk gibberish, Shimi."

"Don't call me that, I said. I talk sense," Simon said. "I am not your Shimi, nor your love, nor anyone's. I am a lost soul. I must find myself before I cleave to a wife."

Simon sighed and sensed new air going into a deeper place than before, a place unexplored.

"God loves you," Bracha said. "He accepts English."

"I don't love myself."

"Oy," Bracha whimpered. "*Oy va-voy.*"

Simon rose from the plastic chair. He waved goodbye to Bracha. She hid her face in her napkin.

His feet headed north on Bethlehem Road and he followed them. The day was young and full of promise. His walk became bouncy after he crossed the railroad tracks. Even though he was unsure of where he was going or what he would call himself or what books he would read, he invited God, the Holy One, Blessed be He, and the Evil Inclination to join him on his journey, if they so desired. They would have to learn how to get along with each other, though, or he'd kick them both out. For the first time in his life, Simon put his faith in Simon, whoever that turned out to be.

Ovadia, Falafel Shack

My social worker says if I make trouble with the
city inspector, he won't let me sell shawarma. I
ask you, what's a falafel stand without shawarma?
Not everyone loves falafel, even mine, even when I
throw scraps of fried eggplant and chips on top.
Take Avrami, for instance, across the street.
Sometimes he wants a meat lunch and his wife works
in the store with him. So why shouldn't he eat
meat? The King of Falafel downtown, he sells both,
so why not Ovadia? Is he better than me? I'm King
of Bethlehem Road! He's out to get me, this city
inspector. His second cousin has his eye on my
place. Lots of people have their eyes on my place.
Waiting for Ovadia to drop dead. But I'm not selling, not to nobody. And I'm not dropping dead. I
put my heart and soul into Falafel Ovadia. Who puts
nine balls in a pita? Only Ovadia! Look at these
hands. You see the Formica table there on the sidewalk? I found it in a dump and fixed it up nice. A
few plastic chairs and voilà! The city inspector
says I'm taking over the neighborhood. He wants to
close me down. Just let him try. I'll get Dr. Yarus
and my social worker to write letters: If Mr. Ovadia does not get shawarma, he will have a nervous
breakdown. Ovadia cannot be moved! Ovadia is here
for good! Long live Ovadia!

ANNIE AND TED

The costumes were amazing. One man, who didn't move from the punch bowl all night—imported ginger ale, lemonade, and date honey—came as a shower stall. Tehila's upstairs neighbor, born in Fez, dressed as shawarma. The smell of roasted lamb dripped from her hair. Tehila's friends were all from somewhere else. One guy, trying hard to fit in, came dressed as a sabra, acupuncture needles sticking out of his olive-green face. He spoke only Hebrew.

I was in no mood for partying on that Purim in March 1970, but Tehila, née Terry, my best friend from the gap year, insisted I come. "First God makes you cry," she told me on the Fast of Esther, "then demands joy." It had been an awful month, what with a hijack and a bus blowup, and on March 19, Elitzur, my Tunisian boyfriend, who I assumed would save me from myself, dropped me for a Norwegian.

I costumed as a queen-witch, a combo of the two roles Elitzur had accused me of perfecting. Clearly these were projections from his childhood feelings toward his mother and four older sisters. Around my pointed black hat I balanced a cheap gold tiara.

"The royal witch," Tehila bellowed, welcoming me to the fray.

"Call me Qwitch," I told her, as I poured a bottle of tequila into the punch.

Beyond the bowl, I spied my heroes. Annie and Ted didn't need costumes; they were the real thing. Ted wore the same black suit and top hat he had worn to the Basel conference in 1897. His full dark-brown beard circled his thick lips and trailed to his chest like a carpet. I wanted to crawl on that carpet and kiss those lips, but the night was young. He was more handsome and mysterious in real life than in the postcard over my bed, the one where he's leaning over that bridge in Basel, imagining how to turn reality into dreams. Fortunately, at the party he was sitting on a folding chair. If I had encountered the upright six feet four inches of Herzl, even leaning over a bridge, I would have been intimidated by his enormous presence.

Annie, "Little Miss Sure Shot," stood close to Ted's chair, her hands on her waist, ready for action. She wore her dark-beige pigskin outfit with frills dangling from collar, arms, and boots. Her wavy brown hair, neatly pulled back behind her ears, covered her shoulders. A heavy leather cowboy hat sat on her petite head like an oversized halo. On the left side of her chest hung eight sharpshooting medals, the print too small to read in the hushed light. At the center of her collar shone a gold Magen David that echoed the shine in her eyes. She smelled like a circus tent. Her lips, too, were sumptuous and I wondered if she and Ted were into each other.

Did I miss Elitzur? Not one iota. Did I think of him? Yes. He was seven inches taller than me with no higher education. His Tunisian mother spent eight hours a day in the family's kitchen, a room with no windows the size of our guest bathroom back home in Dayton. In that mini space she prepared *couscous chorba* and *chakchouka*, Tunisian dishes I learned to pronounce and even like. I was, possibly, more in love with the mother than the son. But Elitzur, though handsome and a good dancer, was more interested in my sky-blue passport, "exotic" Ohio accent, and straight blonde hair. Mother and all four sisters had black curly locks.

Annie's intriguing beauty did not come across in the old post-cards I collected. In person she reminded me of my Hungarian grandmother, who never reached five feet. Grandma, too, was distant, always mentally somewhere else. Maybe Buda. Perhaps Pest.

I couldn't believe my luck. Here were the two people in the whole world I worshiped most—Annie, since *Spinning Wheels* in fourth grade, the workbook for learning about American pioneer culture, and Ted, since reading *The Zionist Idea* at twenty-four. Here were two role models of how to lead a meaningful life. One overcame poverty and abuse by perfecting her shooting and the other used words to charm and protect vulnerable Jews. Both loved a good show—costume, lights, action, applause.

When I approached, Annie clicked her heels and curtsied. I knew all about her signature moves. They came at the end of every performance in Buffalo Bill's Wild West Show. In fact, I knew a lot about Annie. I grew up in her shadow, so to speak, as her cabin in the woods, when she was a child, was not far from Dayton. I knew the way she shot at balls while leaning over a chair, for instance. This strange position was probably born from the desire to take revenge on the despicable farmer who raped her as a ten-year-old child after her ma sent her to the poor house. But such interpretations were only for the ears of advanced Annie Oakley fans.

I was honored and amazed that Annie could even stand up straight, what with the hat and all that metal hanging from her chest. Instinctively, I removed my Qwitch cap. Good gracious. I was only an inch or two taller than Miss Oakley. We chatted, in English of course. Annie didn't speak Hebrew, Hungarian, Yiddish, or French. When I told her we were both from Ohio, she smiled, leaning slightly into her holster hip.

"Ohio's a good place to be from." She giggled.

"Glad you guys came," I said. "It's been a lousy month, and here you are, my two favorites at a stupid Purim party."

"I had to get away." Ted talked to Annie's medals. "The racket over there on Mount Herzl. It's enough to raise the dead."

Up close he smelled like a Sacher torte, sweet and tangy. I wanted to lick every inch of him but instead just explained that the racket was Shaare Zedek, the Gates of Righteousness Hospital, building its new state-of-the-art medical complex across the street from his abode. "Should be finished in a year . . . or twelve."

He chuckled and I was glad he had a sense of humor. This never came across in his journal, which I found in a used bookstore on King George Street my first week in Jerusalem.

When he opened his mouth, I saw something that could have been a black sesame seed or a remnant from a spinach *boureka* stuck between his lower back molars. I didn't say anything, didn't want to embarrass him. Just wanted to take in his aura.

"I came on a group tour for Christian women," Annie told Ted, her voice high-pitched and slightly grating. "Decided to stay an extra week. Nice weather you got here." While she talked, her right hand covered the grip of her pistol and her eyes scanned the room. With her left hand she brushed her bangs off her forehead. "Of course, the authorities won't let me perform here. 'Too violent,' they say."

When a short guy dressed as a prune walked by and asked her

to dance—to a fast one with Aretha Franklin belting about no one listening to her—Annie said no, she didn't dance anymore. The prune slid out of hearing range and she told Ted this was her first Purim party. "Anyway, I never dance with anyone but Frank, who has no interest in Israel."

Ted tilted his head, crunched the muscle over the left side of his mustache, and said, "*Was gibt?*"

It took me and Annie a minute to figure that out.

"Frank's back home in Baltimore babysitting Sir Ralph."

"Sir Ralph?"

"Our Saint Bernard."

I was elated at having Annie and Ted all to myself. I didn't even mind that they talked with each other and pretty much ignored me. I was used to being ignored.

Annie and Ted had lots in common. They were the same age, both born in 1860, both loners, both traveling for long periods at a stretch, both Jewish, though Annie insisted Pa didn't give a good doggone about being a Jew.

"Ma was a Quaker," she said, "so the Jewish thing isn't part of my show, if you catch my drift. Never learned a thing Jewish, except when the man who owned the hotel in Cincinnati, where I first beat Frank, taught me kosher. I'm only part Jew."

"Which part?" I piped.

Ted gave me a dirty look, as if I were breaking the rules of European bourgeois decorum. He didn't like Israeli in-your-face blunt.

"My sister told me our great-great-grandmother on my father's side was a Marrano. That's why our name was Moses." Annie took out her shining gold-and-silver revolver from the holster, spit on it, and right there in front of us in the middle of this party, where nothing much was happening besides the punch and Aretha Franklin, polished with the hem of her pigskin skirt what already looked sparkling. This was one gorgeous revolver, with the name of the manufacturer right there on the side: Smith & Wesson. I knew young mothers who didn't give their own babies this much attention.

While sliding the pistol back into her holster, she told Ted that next to her Pa's Winchester over the fireplace in their cabin stood two candlesticks. "Nobody ever used them," she said, raising her voice to a higher squeak. Then she giggled, which reminded me of my father, who always told me to stop giggling—*Get control of yourself, Beth*—clicked her heels, and curtsied again.

It surprised me nobody else at the party took an interest in Annie or Ted. The other single women, including Tehila, seemed more interested in the shower stall. After Annie rejected the prune, no other guys asked her to dance and nobody hit on Ted, maybe due to his height.

I brought Annie and Ted cups of spiked punch.

Finally, Annie asked me something about myself. "What's a Dayton girl like you doing in Jerusalem?"

I told her I was looking for roots, like lots of other Americans back home, but whereas they were looking in San Francisco, I chose Jerusalem. I told her about my job as a cashier at the plant nursery on Bethlehem Road, having been fired from the Biblical Zoo. "A tourist I was guiding had a finger bit off by a donkey. He sued. Threatened to close the place. That sealed my fate." I mentioned my recent breakup with Elitzur, who accused shy, unassuming me of playing the Queen card, as well as the Witch.

More explanations did not satisfy her curiosity about why I left Ohio for Jerusalem.

"Ohio's got everything," she told Ted. "Lakes, rivers, rabbits, raccoons."

Ted's lips tightened into a snarl. Was he angry I wasn't like one of his happy, well-adjusted characters in *Old-New Land*? I felt guilty for disappointing him, and even more so for being unable to explain. He was the last person I wanted to disappoint. Maybe I should have shut up and gotten control of myself, like Dad said.

Annie was interested in hearing about wildlife hunting in Montgomery County, for which, again, I had no satisfying answers, as my family only did indoor sports—Ping-Pong in the basement, Scrabble on the kitchen table. My father was in the knot business—ropes, strings, ribbons, small *shmattes*. A man of no hobbies, only work. The only hunting I had done in Dayton was at Friday-night canteens in seventh grade in the basement of the new rec center of Corpus Christi, while Johnny Mathis sang "Wonderful, Wonderful."

"Once a Buckeye, always a Buckeye," Annie said, despite my silence. She smiled at the punch in her cup.

Annie and Ted schmoozed all night—his plays, her guns, his Jews, her fans, his hats, her medals, His Majesty the Sultan, her Sitting Bull. They led such colorful, rich, and meaningful lives. By the end of the party, I couldn't bear the thought of separating, so I invited them to my place.

Ted and Annie were reluctant to come. I enticed them with *gazoz*. "It's an Israeli must, a first cousin to Kool-Aid . . . and my place was built in '95."

"My best year." Ted stood up after the mention of that glorious year, recalling what a smash his little pamphlet made, especially in the ghettos and shtetls of Eastern Europe and the Pale.

I knew about his fiery Parisian period, when, recovering from the Dreyfus Affair during the heat of June and July, he played with his homeland idea, then a mere pile of papers on his desk with scribbles, deletions, and notes in the margins, when he went out every night to hear Wagner as a respite from working on the document, the pamphlet that six months later would become *The Jewish State.*

"Just for a short visit," Annie said, with an emphasis on "short."

Tehila gave me a big hug as we left the party.

"How did you know who to invite?" I whispered in her ear.

"God works in mysterious ways, darling. He wants you to be happy."

Rehov Mordechai HaYehudi was quiet at one thirty in the morning. Fortunately, some of the streetlamps were still on, so we could see all the broken sidewalks. I pointed out the new deli in the shopping complex on Rehov Esther HaMalka. Annie asked if she could find grits anywhere in the Holy City. "I'd love a decent blintz," croaked Ted.

With pride I walked between Annie and Ted and wondered how I could satisfy their appetites. I threw my Qwitch cap into the overstuffed dumpster at Herzl's vegetable market on the corner of Bethlehem Road. The street was undergoing an "archaeological dig" for a change, which meant the sidewalk, too, was strewn with barriers. I stepped down into the street and gave the narrow sidewalk to my heroes, offering the honor and respect they deserved.

"After each paving," I explained to the not-so-curious Annie and Ted, "some municipal department, the electric company or telephone company, remembers that it forgot to lay a certain wire in exactly the same place that was just dug up last month and paved, so the road is in a continuous state of 'archaeological dig.'"

They couldn't have cared less. Annie never took her right hand off her beloved Smith & Wesson. Ted, towering above us, looked down the road, way into the future.

I pointed out the plant nursery in the front yard of 62 Bethlehem Road, corner of Gid'on, where I worked.

As we passed Shlomo's lottery stand, a street cat jumped at us from behind the kiosk. Annie flipped her pistol. I screamed. Annie aimed. Thank God she didn't shoot the fat cat. All I needed were neighbors calling the police and some young cop driving up the road, shooting at Annie below her knees, handcuffing her, grabbing her baby, her gun, and taking it and the girl to the Kishle prison for questioning . . . *You're who?*

Ted told me to calm down, just like my father and Elitzur used to say. "Get control of yourself, kid." I never wanted to control myself, but I liked having Ted pay me some attention, even if he forgot my name. "Breathe deeply," he told me.

"I see why people call you Messiah," I said, "and King of the Jews and Moses." A pianissimo breath left my mouth. This Herzl had a definite kind streak.

Annie twirled her beloved on her right forefinger and threw it to her left forefinger as if she were in a yo-yo playoff. She flung it back into her holster as soon as she realized the moving object that caused the initial reaction was a neighborhood cat and not some rattler, bat, wild boar, or who knows what else she imagined roaming the night streets of Jerusalem.

We walked toward my home in silence. In front of the house on the corner of Bethlehem Road and Shimshon, with the garden of olives and figs, Ted said to Annie, *"Tres jolie ici, n'est-ce pas?"*

They'll always have Paris, I thought.

I was glad Ted liked Baka. Maybe he would consider moving. There was a cemetery nearby on Valley of Ghosts Street, noisy, but not as noisy as Mount Herzl. He could do the research and decide for himself if he wanted to be part of a home for Evangelical Christians. He didn't need my advice.

That year I lived in a stone building on the corner of Yiftach and Bethlehem Road. The house was built in 1895 by an Armenian Christian from the Old City of Jerusalem. My entrance was from Yiftach. Between the street and the door stood a giant kermes oak tree. When we approached, I noticed the lower branches of the tree were covered with fake shaving cream.

"Is this Israeli snow?" Annie asked.

I explained that teenagers go wild on Purim, spraying fake shaving cream at people and trees. "It's a mitzvah to be happy."

"But to destroy property?" Herzl said with disbelief.

In the dim light from the road, I took out the brass key from my purse, put it in the lock, leaned against the door, and, twisting the key, pushed it open. The irregular flagstone floor was filthy. I was sorry I hadn't washed it during the past month of tears, and I hoped the cockroaches in the kitchen and bathroom would not startle Annie and Ted. We walked into my bedroom.

The pale green walls of the vaulted room embarrassed me for some reason. I hoped my guests would focus on the intricate turquoise cross-stitching on the quilts covering the two single beds. My Hungarian grandmother's handiwork. Maybe this would make Herzl feel at home. There was enough room for all of us if they wanted to stay the night, for in the adjoining living room, with its twelve-foot-high vaulted ceiling and walls two feet thick, was a Simmons Hide-A-Bed.

Annie and Ted sat down on either end of the Hide-A-Bed couch without commenting on the beauty or uniqueness of my rental. I excused myself and walked into the kitchen to take down three glasses. Why hadn't I dried them better? Who knew when important guests would arrive? Hadn't Thomas Paine dropped in last Independence Day? And what about Emily Dickinson's unannounced visit for tea and rugelach on Memorial Day?

Fortunately, the bottle of grape concentrate in the fridge was only half empty and the gray contraption that made fizzy water was full. I poured three glasses of *gazoz*.

When I entered the living room with the drinks, my guests were talking to each other but both looking through the enormous window at the kermes oak outside.

"I need your help," Ted said, as if he were still on a mission.

Annie took out her pistol from its holster, spit on it, and polished it again with her pigskin skirt, her eyes locked to her lap. Granted, it was a beautiful piece of machinery. Even a pacifist like me could appreciate that, but her dependence on it seemed extreme.

"One of your plays, I saw it in Paris," she said in a monotone screech. "You should stick to essays."

Ted blushed on that part of his face not covered by hair. "I saw your show in Paris too," he said, turning toward her. "One night I'd go to *Tannhäuser*, the next night I'd buy a ticket to Buffalo Bill's Wild West Show. I wanted to figure out why your show was so successful, so I went a few times."

"Did you figure?" Annie slowed down her polishing and her concentration moved to her ears.

By now I was sitting in the rocking chair near the passage between the bedroom and living room. Rocking away, I held on to every word.

"It's because of you, Miss Oakley." Ted looked straight at her when he spoke and even pointed his index finger and thumb at her, the way children play when they shoot an imagined gun. You could tell he wanted her to look at him, but Annie kept her eyes on her revolver. "You're the star of that show, Annie, not Buffalo Bill. And not Sitting Bull," he said, inching closer. "Granted, the Indians are superb, like nothing we have in Europe, but you, you are an artist. You understand theater, drama. This is what I teach my Jews before each congress. The show, the lights, costume, staging." Ted paused and took a sip of *gazoz*. "But you should get those goddamned Cossacks out of the act."

She looked at him now for the first time, amazement in her dark eyes. She put her polished gun down on the glass coffee table, gently, as if it were a newborn who had just fallen asleep. Gunless, her hands looked forlorn.

"Just local color, Mr. Herzl," she said. "Not to be taken seriously." Then, instead of leaving the baby there to rest, she picked it up again, put it back in its holster, and took a sip from the dirty glass. "I'm glad you appreciated the show. Buffalo Bill's the real genius." She swished the juice in her mouth as if she were rinsing after brushing her teeth and then spit it back in the glass. "I'm just a lucky girl with a gun," she said. She looked around the foreign room, studying its contours and recessed barrel-vaulted windows. "Some people, like you, Mr. Herzl, write and organize and create to survive . . . I shoot . . . It's like breathing."

Ted nodded and stood up, dominating the room with his presence, his head only halfway to the ceiling. I kept rocking. I couldn't stop rocking; like a Sufi dancer I was moving into trance mode. The harder I rocked the more I thanked God for bestowing this opportunity on me—to experience the presence of greatness.

Ted walked over to the window opposite the couch and leaned into its deep alcove. Then he turned around suddenly toward the couch. "I need your help, Annie." He took off his top hat and flicked it onto the coffee table, where it landed exactly between the two glasses of *gazoz*.

I was aghast at his timing and focus. I was startled when he began to unbutton his collar button. Seeing the dark hair on his chest below his beard made my lower body tingle. Jeepers, he was a handsome man. Again, I wanted to kiss him, a deep French kiss, but I kept right on rocking.

Annie looked at him as if she knew what was coming.

"I spoke to Wilhelm in Constantinople," Ted said in his lowest register. "Wilhelm promised he would help us procure the Holy Land."

Ted's eyes deepened, as if he held millions of starving Jewish mouths there, all pleading for chicken soup, kosher or non-. He turned to look at the oak tree, defaced with shaving cream, alone, surrounded by darkness. When he turned back to Annie, his whole face was covered with sadness. "I met Wilhelm a few weeks later on Street of the Prophets in Jerusalem. He reneged."

The fridge in the kitchen offered a sad hum.

"Just like that," he continued. "One day he is saving the Jewish People and the next, nothing. *Rien. Gornisht. Nichts.*"

The upper branches of the oak tree rubbed against the panes.

"Annie," he said, larghissimo, "a piece of land is all we need."

Annie shot back with her own Wilhelm story. "I met the guy once in Mainz when he was still Crown Prince. Conceited fellow, as I recall. Insisted I shoot the lit tip off his cigarette, so I stood him over by Frank and put a holder in his mouth. The guy didn't know what hit him when this cigarette dangled from his mouth without the ash. Used my .32-20 Winchester, as I recall."

I stopped rocking. Could it be that Annie would not be moved to help Wolf Theodor, Benjamin Zev, Ted, Herzl—this idealistic, royal man of many names, a man who embodied all the beauty, intelligence, and culture of the Austro-Hungarian Empire, who had even sat with the prime minister of Austria *eleven* times, the prime minister, who was only one step below the great Emperor Franz Joseph himself, Franz Joseph, who was always "good to the Jews," to quote Hungarian Grandma, who called him Ephraim Yossele? How could Annie not help this writer turned political activist who had met with His Majesty the Sultan of Turkey, a few Rothschilds, a Schiff, German, Russian, and British royalty—nay, even a Pope!—and who would have met with Abraham Lincoln, that other Moses, had the poor fellow not been shot at the play?

"I can't afford to wait," he said, speaking even louder. "The Cossacks are killing my people. I need your help, Miss Oakley. Talk to McKinley. Please."

His passion brought tears to my eyes.

Annie took out her polished pistol and placed it on the coffee table next to Ted's hat. Now she looked into his sad, Hungarian eyes and I thought she might respond in the affirmative.

Instead, she picked up her pistol. A shot was fired, whether intentionally or not. The bullet scraped the vaulted ceiling, chipping the pale paint, whirled down, and punctured the glass coffee table, causing it and the glasses to explode in all directions like firecrackers, grape *gazoz* shpritzing onto the walls and Hide-A-Bed and cold stone floor, from whence said bullet bounced off, up, down, and into my left knee.

"*Ouch!*" I screamed and put my hands on my leg to hold the

poor thing together, blood spilling out. I leaned over in pain. "You shot my knee."

Annie sat on the couch as if nothing had happened. Ted barely glanced at his ruined damp hat on the floor.

"Mr. Herzl," she said, slowing down and lowering her voice, "you're asking me to talk to the president of the United States of America."

"That I am," he said.

"Wait a minute," I screamed, looking at Annie. "You shot my knee." Now I turned to Ted. "My blood's on the floor."

"McKinley's a busy man, Mr. Herzl."

"I know," said Ted. "But my people are homeless and suffering. You are my last hope."

He stared at Annie, her past successes pinned to her chest, glittering in the light coming in from the lone streetlamp. Annie stared at Ted, his fear of failure covering his face like a mask. I felt like throwing my brass candlesticks at them, but I was afraid to move.

"Help me," I moaned. "I'm one of those people and *I'm* suffering."

I tried to stand up, but the pain was too much.

"Always like to help poor girls, Mr. Herzl," she went on. "Always give a few cents to the poor things hanging around my dressing room door in Baltimore, but your request, Mr. Herzl . . . you want me to save a whole people. I don't know the first thing about this politic business. I just shoot flying clay ducks, one two three four up to seven, just like that, back to the ducks, counting them in a mirror I hold in my left hand. I'm not even a real Jew . . . only my father's side, way back. Isn't there a statute of limitations? You Jews make so much out of names. So what if Pa once appeared in a godforsaken census as Jacob Moses?"

Ted interrupted, almost shouting. "My people need a home, Annie." He stretched his arms toward her, now both fingers taking aim. "I need your help, Annie. Oklahoma. Wyoming. Nebraska. I'll settle for a Dakota."

"What about me," I said, managing to pick up a corner of a broken glass and throwing it at Ted's beard, but missing.

"Calm down," Ted said, but he was looking at Annie, not at me.

She stood up and walked toward him. "I know what that's like, Mr. Herzl. I was homeless after Pa died."

I collapsed onto the floor and pressed my fingers into my throbbing knee. I knew about that night in 1866 when Annie's father arrived home during a snowstorm, sitting in the driver's seat of the carriage, three-fourths frozen by the time he opened their front door, dying in the cabin a few days later. I knew about her being sent to the county poorhouse, then slaving for the wicked farmer who probably raped her over a chair. I knew she sent all her money back to her ma so they could keep their cabin in the woods. I knew all about it, but I no longer cared. I closed my eyes and sank into the stone floor.

"Why do you think McKinley would see me?" Annie said.

"He's from Canton," Ted replied.

"Once a Buckeye, always a Buckeye."

I floated in darkness near a tree. No. It was a stump, covered by a plexiglass box. I had seen it once on my pilgrimage to Motza. The stump of the cedar that Benjamin Zev planted. November 2, 1898. But why a stump? Had anti-Zionist hoodlums destroyed the tree? Did the Jewish Agency rush to preserve a stump, the holy stump of holy Herzl's tree? Of course they did. How else could future generations of homeless Jews recall the great and regal, the profound and prophetic visionary of the Jewish State?

Clapping, people were clapping, or was it kids screaming? I opened my eyes. From the floor, filthy with blood, *gazoz*, and glass, I saw fresh shaving cream being sprayed onto the kermes oak. No giant, no cowgirl. No pleading, no pistol. *Gornisht. Nichts. Klum.*

I moaned. This was no dream and there was no help. I was on my own, all of me on my own shoulders. In order to stand, I had to shake off this tyranny of the past. I had thought we could all live together, Herzl, Oakley, and me, under a fig tree, and not be afraid, but I was way off. Would I have to leave and start all over again in Dayton, Lorain, or Toledo?

Could I stay in Jerusalem without my heroes?

If I willed it, maybe it could be.

SETTLING DOWN

Build there a house in Jerusalem
and dwell there.

1 KINGS 2:36

LAW OF RETURN

Boaz brought me to see this place the day after eleven terrorists landed on the beach south of Haifa and killed thirty-five people. I remember the number because one of them was a friend of my best friend. This was the first time I knew someone who knew someone who was killed in a terrorist attack. It gave me a weird sense of belonging, even though I came to "build and re-build," not to kill and be killed.

Now Stein's prodigal son was returning from New York, so I had to get out of my flat in two weeks. I was done with rentals, having moved twice in three years. Surely rebuilding demanded owning my own place. Boaz parked across the street in front of the school for what they then called "retarded children." The school looked like a prison, all the windows covered with chicken wire. He pointed at number 49. The first things I noticed were the two date palms in the front. A grape vine entangled the two trunks. The palms reached beyond the second floor and seemed like they had been there for decades. I wondered who planted them.

Baka was run-down in those days, with youth gangs hanging out on Bethlehem Road at the corners of Yehuda and Levi. Zila, my neighbor in Rehavia, was aghast that I even considered looking at a place here. "Old Arab houses full of new immigrants?" she said. "Go to one of the new neighborhoods—Ramat Eshkol or Gilo. The schools in Baka are lousy." As if I cared then. I wasn't even married.

Boaz assured me Baka was changing. A family from Chicago had recently bought a flat at 43 Bethlehem Road. They were putting in "*fency* new windows." A British woman was renovating at the end of Rehov Yocheved. Across from 49, the pharmacy had been sold to a French pharmacist. He was planting rose bushes out front, after thirty years of neglect. "Signs of gent-cation," Boaz said, skipping syllables.

He led me into the entrance hall of the building. Mailboxes were falling off their hinges, paint peeling from the walls. It was clear the tenants didn't care about the building. They were immigrants who had been settled here after the War of Independence, Boaz explained. Two families lived here—one Moroccan, the other Iraqi. They had bickered since 1950 but had finally, after twenty-eight years, agreed to sell the flat as one unit.

Boaz knocked on the door. I stood in the hallway, waiting, wishing Stein hadn't kicked me out. A woman with an orange kerchief on her head opened the door. Inside, pandemonium. Two little kids fought in the corner. Another woman with a kerchief battered raw chicken breasts on the marble counter in the kitchen with one of those wooden mallets. I had never seen *that* before. Oil cackled on a stovetop and splattered the walls. A man yelled for toilet paper from the bathroom. Back then the flat had only one kitchen and one toilet for the two families. Four or five children sat on the floor around a huge silver tray covered with uncooked orange lentils. Arms tangled in the orange sea, they fished for stones, shouting, "I got one, I got one!"

The floor was gorgeous. Even now in this heat, it remains cool. On that first day, a late-afternoon sun cast shadows from the grapevine outside onto the painted vines on the tiles. It felt like the whole house had sprung from a vineyard. Tendrils wove their way through the rooms. Grape leaves undulated on the floor. It reminded me of the passage *I shall take a vine out of Egypt and plant it.*

Boaz led me through the maze of one messy room after another. He said nothing of the meter-and-a-half-thick walls, the arched entranceways, the huge windows and high ceilings, higher than anything in the new apartments being built in Ramat Eshkol or Gilo. True, the place needed a renovation to make the two separate apartments one. And apparently it came with headaches. Boaz told me the upstairs neighbors used the garden opposite the kitchen window. Every house in Baka, apparently, had legal issues among the residents, because the garden surrounding the house was common property of all the residents. All that seemed secondary. I was entranced.

Boaz understood I liked the place, despite its shortcomings, and told me to make an offer quickly. The Moroccan neighbor might renege. "Catch him while he's hot," he advised, touching my arm and smiling his warm, inviting smile.

That night I couldn't get this floor—and Boaz—out of my mind. The next day I talked to my friends. They all said I was crazy. "The neighborhood's a slum," Zila said. "A house is like your soul. You must be careful with your soul, Laura. Why do you think it's only twenty thousand dollars? No self-respecting Anglo-Saxon Jew would live there."

The next day I called Boaz and said yes. Something deeper than reason pulled me here. Boaz arranged everything. In six weeks the families were out. Boaz gave me the key the day before we were scheduled to meet at the lawyer's office to sign the contract. I wanted to see the place empty. An hour before the meeting, I came here. That's when everything began to change.

It was June 6, exactly 4:00 p.m. I remember because the news was just beginning and I turned it off as I parked across the street. I walked up the stairs and opened the door with the key Boaz had given me. It was easy. I closed the chain latch behind me. The silence was magical. The undulating floor took my breath away again. I felt not alone, as if a living land were breathing below me. The flat looked larger, of course, since it was empty. Dark-green stencils of grape leaves, which I hadn't noticed on my first visit, wrapped the room at its waist. Strips of pale tan paint from the wooden window frames lay on the floor. Water gurgled through a pipe somewhere. I went to jiggle the hanging chain in the bathroom, but the noise didn't stop.

I stood right here, in the middle of this room, closed my eyes, and turned in a circle. Once, twice. I spread out my arms, threw my head back, and turned. My arms stretched out toward the stenciled walls towering above me. I turned until dizziness felt like home and in this turning I embraced the room, the flat, this land, my life. My hair whirled around me. "Ahhhhh," I hummed, ingesting my new world. I turned until I got so dizzy I had to sit down, cross-legged, and bury my head in my lap.

Soul indeed. I thought of the midrash: Jerusalem is the center of the world and the Temple is the center of Jerusalem and the Holy of Holies is the center of the Temple. At that moment, for the first time in my life, I felt I was in the center of the world. No, I felt I *was* the center of my world. You must understand, boys, this was an unusual feeling for a new immigrant, always aware she was an outsider.

It was for this sense of belonging I had moved to Jerusalem in the first place, and it was this feeling I longed for many years after that day. I tried to recapture it when I took possession and moved in, dancing in the middle of this room when I was alone. I longed for that feeling after I married Boaz. I tried to recreate it after Aryeh was born. I would hold him at my chest and together we waltzed among the grape vines in the middle of this room.

On that June day I was 100 percent sure this house would be mine, that it would shield me from loneliness, depression, estrangement. I would renovate and in that process be rebuilt. On that day, an hour before I was to sign the contract, I felt renewed.

Then somebody knocked on the door.

At first I didn't pay it any heed, thinking it was one of the sounds an old house makes. After all, nobody lived here. The house was a liminal no-man's-land—empty time and space between two tenants.

The knocks grew stronger, definitely at the front door, not some pipe in a wall. I got up from the floor, still dizzy and ecstatic from my dance. I unlocked the latch, opened the door slightly, leaving the chain in place.

Between the door and its frame I saw a man, a gentleman, actually, in his fifties or sixties. He reminded me a little of Teddy Kollek, the mayor of Jerusalem, the refined paunch. He wore a gray suit, odd on a summer day. A gold chain dangled from the breast pocket. He even wore a tie, green, the same shade as the leaf stencils. He looked like an official clerk from the Mandate. His fist hung suspended at his chest, as if ready to knock again. Or— and for a second I felt a flicker of fear—to attack.

"Miss, I did not mean to startle you," he said. "I have been waiting . . ."

His English was beautiful, British English. We shared something, even though I knew right away he was an Arab.

"I have been waiting..."

"Who are you waiting for?" I asked.

He said he wanted to come in. I knew I should close the door in his face, pretend he did not exist, hope that he would walk away, but something in his eyes looked so pathetic. This was no terrorist. This was a man my father's age, maybe, a man on whose face all the letters of sadness vied for space. Beads of sweat lined the ridge above his eyebrows.

I unhooked the chain and opened the door. He walked in.

"My name is Abu Yusuf," he said and cleared his throat. He asked for a drink of water.

It was hot outside, though cool and comfortable in the house. I wondered how he had gotten here. Bus? Cab? Did he own a car? I walked into the kitchen, aware that I shouldn't go deeper into the flat, shouldn't turn my back on him, not because it was impolite. At that time Arabs stabbed Jews on the streets of Jerusalem, so why couldn't it happen in this room?

There was one filthy glass in the sink. I rinsed it and brought him water. He took a few sips and then pulled a white kerchief from his pants pocket, wiped his brow, and cleared his throat.

"My father owns this house," he said.

It has been almost twenty years since that visit. Those words, *My father owns this house*, rather than fading, have grown stronger, especially now. I cannot get them out of my head. *My father owns this house.*

"What do you mean your father owns this house," I said, indignant, surprised, and a little scared. "In an hour I am buying the house from the owners—a Moroccan and an Iraqi Jew—for the sterling equivalent of twenty thousand dollars. I'm afraid you're mistaken. Sir, the government of Israel declared this house abandoned property in 1948."

He closed his eyes and again wiped the sweat from his brow. I continued talking.

"Then Amidar and the Israel Lands Authority took it over. They resettled immigrants here in 1950 and the immigrants bought the flat from Amidar. I saw the papers. I saw the stamps. Now they are selling it to me." The more I talked, the more upset I became. "In an hour, sir, I will meet the legal owners at the lawyer's. In an hour this flat will be mine. How could your father own it?"

"Amidar? What is this Amidar?" he said, as if I were talking gibberish. "Abandoned? Who told you that? You think this house was abandoned? Do you know what happened that night?" He looked at me with sad eyes that made me feel foolish, all my facts irrelevant.

I thought of what Zila had told me one night after I had come home from a Peace Now demonstration. "What do you know? You get off a plane from London where you have everything and you think you can make peace? You have no idea what these people did to us. What they do to us still."

"No," I said to the man, "I have no idea what happened that night."

He stared at me in this room, his burly hands holding his damp handkerchief at the side of his body. There was no time to discuss this and no place to sit. I looked at my watch, assuming he would get the message and leave, but he just stood here, wrapped in quiet wrath.

"My father built this house in 1928," he said. His voice was clear like the first rains of a flood. He walked into what had been a children's bedroom. Silence illumined his sentence like the quiet after gunfire.

I followed him into the room and said something to emphasize that his father had built the house before 1948. I wanted to show him that the rules had changed after the war. He didn't respond. I asked him where he lived now.

"Ramallah," he said. I asked if he lived with his father and he said his father died two days before the war . . . I didn't understand. '48? '67? Which war was he talking about? He sensed my uncertainty and said the June War.

Israelis were celebrating the anniversary of that war that week, rejoicing in the miracle that some ascribed to God and others to paratroopers.

"He built this house with his own hands," he said, putting his handkerchief into his pocket and moving over to the walls to touch the stencils. Were they his father's doing? "My father and mother planted those date palms out front, one for fertility and one for everlasting life. One for my sister and one for me."

He walked around the flat and returned to this room, where a few minutes earlier I had been dancing. I followed him. He told me his father started to build the second floor in July '46. "I moved in with my wife in January of '48."

I didn't want to hear any more. It was 4:18 p.m. He walked into a second bedroom. I followed him.

"By April it became too dangerous for Arabs to stay in Baka," he said, "even though it was our neighborhood. We built it, every house on this street. On April 24 a Jewish man came to the door during the fighting and screamed at my father to get out by morning."

I didn't know anything about this. I thought the Arab leaders had told the local Arabs to leave until the fighting was over. Then they would return "on the dead bodies of the Jews" and ransack their homes. Now this Abu Yusuf, who had appeared out of nowhere, was telling me his family had been kicked out by a Jew.

I had a feeling he was twisting the facts, but I didn't want to get into an argument. I started walking toward the door. He walked toward the kitchen. I told him I had to leave.

"My father did not want to leave," he said, touching the walls of the kitchen with his hands. "I promised him we would return when the fighting ended. He slapped me. I will never forget that night. 'A man does not abandon the house he built,' my father said. I had to carry him out of this house over my shoulder. All the time he is saying, 'A man does not abandon the house he built. This is my house. This is my house.' He was crying. I had never seen my father cry before that night. I had to carry him away, my own father, over my shoulder. Can you imagine this?"

I did not want to imagine this. I wanted him to get out of my kitchen. I wanted him to go, so I could make my appointment and buy the flat. I wanted my own piece of property, so no landlord could ever kick me out again.

"He wailed like a child all the way to Ramallah. For the rest of the war and for years after, he cried: 'My house, my house, a man does not abandon his house.'"

I reached the front door. His story moved me. It reminded me of what Zila had told me. In Abu Yusuf's story, I saw how a house could be the manifestation of a soul. If that was true, then the floors and the walls of this flat I was buying at five o'clock were infused with the soul of Abu Yusuf's father.

"Could you please leave now," I said.

Abu Yusuf stood under the arch leading into the kitchen. He looked out the window facing the backyard and then turned to me. "On my father's deathbed he made me promise to return. I came here on June 30 after the June War, but the people did not let me in. Every year after that on June 6, the day my father died, I come back to his house, but the people never let me in. You are the first person who let me into my father's house."

My stomach clenched. I was angry at myself for letting him in and angry at him for making me sad. I opened the front door and told him I had to go. He walked slowly over to the front window as if he owned the place and stared at the two date palms.

When he turned toward me I saw tears on his cheeks.

I opened the door wider. It is a land that devours its inhabitants, I thought, shuddering.

"I'm terribly sorry," I said. "I have to go."

He looked at me with an expression that pierced all the joy I had felt only fifteen minutes earlier. I realized at that moment that I was buying much more than seventy square meters in Baka. I was paying for a painful legacy, a complicated history that began before I was born.

"I'm really sorry," I said again. "Would you mind leaving? I have to get to the lawyer's."

"Sure," he said. "My family is used to being kicked out by Jews."

Kicked out by Jews? Even today, twenty years later, when I think of those words, I shudder. Especially now that I know what Aryeh did right before he was shot. How could this Abu Yusuf implicate me in his family's story? I was a child in London when all that happened, and there he was putting me in the same role as that man who kicked his family out of this house in '48.

I clenched my arms with both hands to quiet the shudder. He walked by me without looking in my eyes. I took the front-door key out of my pocket and followed him out. Then I turned around and put the key in the lock. I jiggled it, but couldn't lock the door. I looked at my watch. It was already 4:45 p.m. I'd be late. I felt Abu Yusuf's breath on my back. His breathing made me more nervous, so I jiggled the key harder and began to curse in a whisper and all the time I felt his breath on my back and heard him thinking, *This foreigner, this new immigrant, she doesn't even know how to lock the door.*

"Here," he said, "I'll show you."

I moved aside and he put one heavy hand on the key and the other on the door handle. He moved the key gently. The door locked. He took the key out of the lock and held it cupped in his hands. Then he drew his hands to his heart and closed his eyes and I thought he was saying a prayer. When he opened his eyes, he walked past me toward the stairs that lead to the street. Would he leave with the key?

I put my hand on his arm. "Abu Yusuf," I said, "I am so sorry for the pain this house has caused you." No matter what the facts were and even though it was not my fault and even though I was celebrating the victory of another war, I was sorry for him.

"There are no victors in war," he said. "There is only pain. Everyone loses."

He handed me the key.

I told him I thought his father was at rest now, now that he had visited his home. He tightened his lips and nodded in agreement. I invited him to return whenever he wanted, to bring his family, but as soon as the words were out of my mouth, I feared I might regret them.

I started walking down the stairs. He followed. When I reached the sidewalk, he was still on the stairs, looking up at the palms that towered above the second floor. "They were this high when he planted them," he said, holding his hand at his knee.

I didn't offer him a ride, but I did extend my hand to say goodbye. He shook it and then clasped my hand with both of his and I felt that he was thanking me for letting him back into his house, even though he didn't say anything. I shook my head in silence, too, and that was the end of our encounter. He walked down Bethlehem Road and disappeared up Rehov Yehuda toward Hebron Road.

I rushed to the lawyer's and bought the flat.

Abu Yusuf never came back and I never looked for him. I never told Aryeh the whole story, not like I'm telling you, but I want you to know. I don't know why. I feel a great comfort when Aryeh's soldiers sit here with me on this floor, the floor I love, the floor where Aryeh learned to crawl.

I've tried to piece together your accounts of what happened that night in Ramallah. There was so much confusion, screaming, fighting, so many contradictory versions of who went where when. Even if my version doesn't mesh with what some of you told me, this is the story I will take with me to the grave.

I understand that your platoon was supposed to be in Jenin that night, but at the last minute Aryeh told you that you were being sent to Ramallah. You didn't know why. I can only wonder if he knew anything more, beyond the immediate task of taking over the apartment buildings and providing a watch from the roofs. He split you into small units, each unit taking over a different apartment house. The house you went to with Aryeh was divided into seven apartments. The top-floor apartment was opposite the entrance to the roof, which was locked.

You did what you were supposed to do, cleared out each apartment by sending everyone in it to the ground-floor apartment. You did this methodically, as Aryeh had trained you, one apartment at a time, so not everyone would be in the stairwell together. After midnight he sent one of you to help the soldier guarding the ground-floor apartment, now full of crying babies, angry parents, scared children and grandparents. Everything went smoothly, until you reached the last apartment, on the top floor, opposite the entrance to the roof. A family with five children and a grandfather lived there. The grandfather held a two-year-old child wrapped in a sheet. The child was crying and the grandfather put him over his shoulder. It's not clear if the baby had a fever or was just scared by all the noise of soldiers bursting into his house in the middle of the night. The old man showed strong opposition to the procedure, which apparently—and none of you knew this until that moment—had been carried out in the same building only three nights earlier. The old man ranted and cursed you in Arabic. One of you pushed him and he fell onto a glass coffee table, still holding the baby. The table broke. Aryeh got angry at you. He offered to help the old man stand up and take the child downstairs. He pushed his M16 to his back and offered the old man a hand. The old man brushed it off and spit at him, the baby screaming.

Once the apartment was cleared, four of you stayed there, collapsing from exhaustion on the living room couch. You all mentioned an elegant samovar from Damascus next to the television. You defrosted some pitas that the family had in the freezer and ate them. Your supplies were supposed to arrive the next morning. You were tired and hungry. You talked about going home for Shabbat and the food your mothers would make for you —stuffed onions, *kubbeh* soup, apple cake. One of you bragged that you already had your ticket to India. You shared your dreams about doing nothing but sleeping, drinking, and smoking on the beaches of Goa for at least six months, just to get Ramallah out of your systems. You couldn't wait to get out of here.

Meanwhile, Aryeh let the commanders in the other apartment buildings nearby know that your building was secured. He let you rest, while he walked to the door to the roof and pried it open. He always went first. He would guard for the first hour while you ate and slept.

Two minutes later you heard shots.

You ran toward the door to the roof and saw Aryeh sprawled on the floor, clutching his M16. The bullet split his head. You all mentioned how strange it was that his eyes were open, wide open, staring at the silent sky.

One of you called for a medic and the rest of you started shooting onto the roofs on all the surrounding buildings, until you got the message that soldiers from your platoon were stationed there.

The sniper managed to disappear.

Not everyone sees it the same way, but all during the shiva I've thought about what happened that night in Ramallah, about Aryeh's small gesture of kindness in the midst of all that horror, about the anonymous sniper waiting in the darkness to ambush an Israeli soldier.

This wicked dance goes on, breaking our hearts, polluting our souls.

Sit with me a little longer, boys. Please. You, who were Aryeh's men, are now my boys. Stay. Let's try to remember some of the good times.

WEDDING DRESS

The lace scratches Efrat's cheeks as Tanya pulls the dress over Efrat's head.

"Careful, Tanya. That hurts."

Tanya chuckles. "You are too sensitive, my dear. This is the softest, most beautiful wedding dress in Jerusalem. A dress for an angel. Everyone sees, wants to touch. 'Who is the bride?' they ask."

Efrat steps out of her white heels and slips into her Birkenstocks. "That makes me nervous," she says. "Did any of your brides ever run away?"

"Doubts, sure. Run, no. After the wedding there's a lifetime of doubts."

Tanya laughs at her own joke, but Efrat is not laughing. This is her third wedding, her third *possible* wedding. The first one, Yitzhak canceled three weeks before the ceremony. Something about his mother's astrologer. The second one, Amos canceled two days before the chuppah. Efrat wasn't sure who had the cold feet.

Efrat gives Tanya a hug before she takes out her checkbook.

"Monday at three, *maideleh*, my angel. The dress will be waiting for you."

~~⨉~~

Outside, August heatwaves swerve above Bethlehem Road. Bus 21 scoots by with a honk, followed by empty cabs. Efrat longs for her to-do list to be over. She crosses the street to the post office to buy seventy stamps for the thank-you notes. She and Oren made post-cards from a photo of themselves covered in mud at the Dead Sea. On the back: *Thanks for a Once in a Lifetime Wedding.* Since then, she has been obsessing about their choice. Why not victorious climbers on top of Masada? Why not lovers enjoying yoga in Ein Gedi? What was she thinking during those heavenly days of laughter and bliss? Now, during this precarious time before the wedding, one of them could still bail.

Fatma kneels Bedouin-style between the two mailboxes in front of the post office, one yellow, one red. Her long black dress with the red hand-embroidered bodice covers her legs, as well as part of the sidewalk.

"*Kif?*" Fatma smiles and asks.

Efrat bends down and extends her hand. Fatma cups Efrat's hand in hers, kisses it, then holds it close to her heart. "I miss you and I miss your stairs," she says in Hebrew, showing her three gold molars.

"Are you coming to the wedding?" Efrat asks.

"Inshallah."

"Show the invitation at the roadblock," she reminds Fatma.

Fatma places some *za'atar* in a piece of old Hebrew newspaper, folds it, and pushes it into Efrat's hand. "Makes him strong in bed," she says, winking.

"Tuesday. Remember."

"*Allahu Akbar,*" Fatma says, slicing a fresh fig. She hands Efrat half and puts the other half into her mouth. "Fruit for lovers."

The line to the clerk in the ground-floor post office almost encircles the building. Efrat decides to return on Monday, before she picks up the dress.

At home she unrolls her yoga mat, spreads it on the living room rug, lies down on her back, does a few twists, and easily moves into the plow position. With her legs behind her head and her arms next to her body, she thinks of Oren. They met in October at Ofra's 7:00 a.m. yoga class at Ramat Rachel. By December they were living together; in March they decided on an August wedding. He was thirty-nine, never married; she was thirty-four. *Bashert* was the word Raphael, Oren's father, used the first time he met Efrat. "Just like your late mother and me," he said, patting Oren on the head, Oren smiling his shy smile.

With her toes spread like a fan on the floor behind her, Efrat wonders if her dress will keep her warm at Bustan Abu Ghosh. What if it's windy? Maybe they should have chosen an indoor option. They chose the last Tuesday in August for the big day because Tuesday earned a "*very* good" in the biblical creation story. Efrat needed all the support she could muster. She couldn't believe Oren would actually stick around and go through with the ceremony. A job offer would come up in Berlin. His father would die. He'd get scared of committing and fly to India.

She lifts her legs into the air into the candle position.

Already on the way back to Jerusalem from Abu Ghosh, he had started with his reservations. Maybe it was too far for his father in Haifa. Or too steep. Did she know anyone who had worked with Dan at the Mighty Grill Restaurant and Catering Company?

Keeping her own doubts safely at her side like an obedient puppy, she had begun looking for the right rabbi. Oren had gone to a religious school as a child, but now he was totally secular and insisted on a young, open-minded rabbi, one of the under-thirty-five-year-olds who offered the secular community an alternative to the old-school rabbis who always showed up two hours late to the chuppah and insisted the bride go to the *mikvah* the night before the wedding.

She lowers her legs slowly. With her back completely on the mat, her head is still spinning. Why did her mother insist on taking her shopping in Milan? When Efrat heard about Tanya, who designed costumes for the Moscow Theatre before her aliyah, she was sold. And she lived nearby on Bethlehem Road. How convenient was that? Her mother was furious, as she reminds her every day. She is so good at making Efrat feel guilty. And before the wedding!

Breathe deeply and let go, she tells herself, fearing it's an impossible task.

On the Shabbat before the wedding, Oren, wearing only his plaid boxer shorts, is standing in the warrior position in the middle of their living room. Efrat looks at him from her downward dog posture. *In three days... Ba'ali, my husband. Maybe Number Three will work.* She lowers herself to the floor, turns onto her back, and tells herself to think positive thoughts. *Delete "maybe."*

Later, upright in the kitchen, Efrat and Oren go over the menu for the thirty thousandth time.

"Dan makes a wicked mushroom with tahini sauce," she says. "Do you think we can cancel the lox on toast?" Efrat isn't sure if this is what she really wants. Maybe she just wants to make conversation and see how Oren reacts. The idea emboldens her.

"What difference does it make?" Oren says, staring into a place beyond the living room window—maybe Mount Zion, or possibly the bedroom of that new woman on the other side of the street, who moved in last month with a Pekingese.

"It makes," she says. "I want everything perfect . . . like my dress."

"Nothing's perfect."

"We're perfect." Efrat knows she's talking rubbish, playing the young innocent bride, though she's neither young nor innocent.

Oren walks over to her and rubs his front against her backside. "This is perfect."

She turns around and opens her mouth for a kiss. Then she asks him to visit Dan on Sunday to cancel the lox.

He licks her gums with his tongue and picks her up for a twirl. She feels a lightness in her head and doesn't know if it's the yoga position she just held for three minutes on the living room floor or love.

On Sundays Oren and Efrat have a routine. They come home early from work, lie on the sofa, and, sipping Merlot from the Galilee, watch reruns of *Soap*. On this Sunday, two days before the wedding, Oren is late because he has gone to Dan at The Mighty Grill to tell him to switch the lox for mushrooms.

After the meeting, Oren calls Efrat to say that Dan wanted to raise the price but he, Oren, took up his warrior pose and *"hakol*

b'seder," says Oren. "But no more changes, sweetheart. This guy's
like a volcano."

Efrat loves this about Oren—his ability to deal with difficult
people, including herself. When she agonizes over calling her father, who lives with a thirty-five-year-old woman in Thailand,
Oren helps her concentrate on her breathing by breathing with
her. Only then can she call.

"I'll pour the wine," Efrat says. As she hangs up the phone,
Efrat wonders why he never married before. If he had such a good
job in San Jose, why did he come back to Israel? *Let it go*, she tells
herself, *let it go*.

She lies down on the couch and waits for Oren to come home
from the *shuk*. A good opportunity to review her to-do list. Tomorrow, she'll buy the stamps for the thank-yous, pick up the
dress from Tanya, and get Abba from the airport. She still isn't
sure if the girlfriend is coming with. Her father loves surprises, but
Efrat made it clear in their last conversation that the girlfriend is
not invited. There have been enough snags and blowups since
June. First the mistake on the invitation: Abo Ghush instead of
Abu Ghosh. Then the photographer's accident in Warsaw in July
and her mother's lump in her left armpit on August 1, the biopsy
results ready on the day after the wedding. And now the canapé
thing. Why couldn't the world just stop for love?

Efrat tucks the Indian pillow under her head. Should they
have chosen India instead of Bali for their honeymoon? She had
never been to either place, nor to Thailand. One day on a bus
when she was in third grade her father told her, "I'm moving to
Thailand." She dozes on the couch, and smiles when she hears
Oren's voice in her head. Now she hears pipes and a ring. The ring
becomes louder and she wakes in a jolt to answer the phone.

It's five thirty. A woman on the other end is asking if she knows Oren Ben-Or.

"Who is this?" She twists her neck to release a kink.

"My name is Nurit." Her voice comes wrapped in gauze.

Efrat wipes her eyes and lowers herself to the cool stone-tiled floor and sits upright with her legs tucked under her buttocks. "Where is he?"

"Did you hear the explosion, ma'am?"

Efrat stopped taking buses when she was eleven. Oren still takes buses in his *davka* mode, his Israeli stiff-necked nothing-can-harm-me mode.

"Did you hear?" the voice on the other end says, now louder, as if Efrat is deaf. "There was a suicide bombing on the number 21."

Efrat puts the receiver on the floor, drops down into the fetal position. She hears the woman's voice shouting, "Are you there? Are you there?"

She pulls the receiver to her ear and takes a long, deep inhale. She wants to hold the air inside and not let it go, not for anyone, but it comes out in spurts from her belly and then from her neck, as if someone is squeezing her.

"He's my fiancé," she says, when all the air is out of her cavity. "Where is he?"

"Can you speak up, ma'am."

She puts the receiver close to her mouth. "What happened?" she whispers. She repeats the question, screaming, "What the fuck happened?" Alarmed, she pushes the phone away, expecting a scream in return, but there is only silence. "I'm sorry," she says slowly. "What happened?"

The voice—Is it Neri? Nurit? Nora?—asks her to come to the hospital now, right now. Hadassah Ein Kerem.

Efrat hangs up and announces to the floor, "We're getting married on Tuesday."

She sits up and begins to dial her mother in Tel Aviv, but after three digits she hangs up. She does not want to hear "I told you so" and "That cursed city." She calls Doda Viv in Rechavia.

"It's Oren," Efrat says.

"Oh God. Dear child. I heard the blast from the kitchen, Frati. I'm coming over."

"No, Doda. I'm going to Hadassah. I'll call you later. Can his father stay with you, still?"

Efrat stands up , despite gravity saying, *Stay, stay*. Within five minutes she is on Bethlehem Road, where a moist dusk wakes her more. The smell of jasmine on the corner makes her cry. Traffic is brisk. Radios blare from open windows. Everyone's listening to up-to-the-minute broadcasts about the latest suicide bombing. The call of sirens from the west like distant jackals tells her many are wounded tonight. Efrat raises her right hand to flag a cab. As she waits, she senses anger bubbling in her gut. A cab stops and she opens the back door. She sees immediately that the driver is an Arab. She hesitates to get inside. The car behind starts honking. "*Yallah, yallah*," cries the cab driver, looking into his rearview mirror. Efrat slides onto the back seat.

"*Yallah, yallah*," she says with vengeance, opening a window. "Hadassah Hospital." Her voice sounds domineering like her mother's.

The driver reaches Yehuda and turns his head toward her. "Which one?"

"What?"

"Which Hadassah, Ma'am?"

"Ein Kerem," she shouts. She wants to add *You idiot, you Arab father of terrorists.*

"Terrible, terrible," the driver says. "Four dead so far."

She cannot believe his reaction is sincere. How could he care? At the Pierre Koenig intersection, traffic is backed up on Rabbi Yohanan ben Zakkai.

The driver turns up the radio to hear the news.

"Turn it off," Efrat screams. "What do you care?"

He makes the left turn onto ben Zakkai and pulls over to the curb.

"Get out, lady," he says, eyes straight ahead. "Find yourself another punching bag."

Efrat apologizes, explains that she's nervous, scared, getting married on Tuesday, the phone call, the bombing, her father's arrival.

"All right, *geveret. B'seder. B'seder.* Relax." He takes a tissue from his glove compartment, gives it to her, and continues driving. She puts the tissue in her purse and watches the oncoming traffic on ben Zakkai. Once Oren told her that during the Roman siege of Jerusalem this ben Zakkai got out of the Old City in a coffin by playing dead. Was it true?

Driver and Efrat sit in a tense silence. Do the four killed include the terrorist? If Oren was killed, a medic from Magen David Adom would have come to tell her. Then a Valium. Good that a nurse called her. Maybe only cuts and scratches.

At Hadassah Hospital ambulances are lined up at the door to the emergency room. Police try to control the crowds of people

83

roaming around screaming "Death to Arabs" by shouting through loudspeakers. Some men push anyone who looks like an Arab orderly. Others try to calm the rabble-rousers. "This man works at Hadassah. Hell, leave him alone."

Efrat hands the driver a fifty-shekel note and does not wait for change. As soon as she exits, a woman with a young child pushes the child into the cab, but when the woman slides onto the back seat and sees the driver is an Arab, she drags her child out and slams the door, cursing. The driver speeds off, empty.

"What do you want?" the clerk asks, as if Efrat is intruding on her work.

"Somebody called. A woman. My fiancé . . ."

"Last name."

"Shapiro."

The woman looks at her list. "Sorry, we have no Shapiro. Try Shaare Zedek Hospital."

"No. That's my name," Efrat says, raising her voice.

"I need the patient's name, ma'am. We go by the patient's name."

"Ben-Or. Oren." She says the name slowly and for the first time gets its meaning: Pine Tree Son of Light. In a flash she understands the hopes his parents had for their first son, born in Israel after the Holocaust.

"Last name?"

Efrat shouts into the glass separating her from the Russian clerk. "His name is Oren Ben-Or? Is that clear?" As she takes the cab driver's tissue out of her purse and places it in her pocket, she notices the clerk's nail polish is blood red.

"Through the door on your left to the right," the clerk says, pushing a green button that opens the door to the emergency room.

Efrat longs for a family. Once she broached the subject, she and Oren spent hours discussing their ideal family. Their son would be a math genius like his father. They laughed about nicknaming him Mispar, number, as in *Ezzeh mispar*, What a number!

The first numbers Oren learned were those embedded in his mother's arm. His mother, pointing to the dark digits, told him, "This is God's telephone number." One day when he was in first grade he dialed the number, but nobody answered. His mother laughed and hugged him until she cried. By Pesach of fourth grade, she was dead. All he had were memories and numbers, which became his obsession and then his profession. Efrat had milked him for these stories on their first dates.

Their daughter, blonde, like Oren was until age five, would become a zoologist. (They couldn't agree on a name.) Their home in Baka would serve as a refuge for stray dogs, cats, and wounded birds.

She is thinking about family now because in the corridor of the ER, families assault her from every direction. Children are screaming for their mothers, fathers are hovering at the foot of the beds of their children, daughters are wiping the brows of elderly parents, wives kissing, husbands praying.

A stench of ammonia mixed with dry blood fills the air. Could it be burning rubber as well? Bodies on gurneys covered with pink Hadassah sheets wait to be pushed somewhere to a background fugue of sobs.

"Someone called me. Efrat Shapiro," she says to the first nurse she sees.

The woman gasps and puts her sandwich in the pocket of her white coat. The uniform has smudges of blood around her hips and for a second Efrat remembers her dress. Tanya will want to know what happened. She'll call her later tonight.

"I'm Nurit," the woman says, swallowing. "Come with me, Efrat." She walks into a small empty room and pulls out a chair for Efrat. "He's lucky," she continues, as she moves her chair opposite Efrat. "His right lung burst from the blast. It's hard to believe he's alive. He was covered in strawberries and blood." She puts her hands in both pockets of her uniform.

Efrat doesn't want to hear any more.

"And wine."

Wine? He didn't need to buy wine. Efrat is furious. How can this woman be talking about her Oren, the man who makes love to her at four in the morning and then again at seven, the man she will call *Ba'ali* on Tuesday night?

"This is lucky?"

"There are four dead," Nurit says, as if pounding this simple arithmetic into Efrat's head. "He is not one of them." She lowers her voice. "This is luck, my dear."

If a bomb goes off on a bus with fifty passengers and four are dead, thirteen seriously wounded, and thirty-three mildly wounded, how many will die within two months? As soon as Jerusalem arithmetic erupts, Efrat tries to erase it.

"He fractured his skull, probably when he landed."

"Landed?" Efrat takes out the tissue from the cab driver. She wants to be like the red mailbox in front of the post office: *Anywhere Except Jerusalem.*

"A medic found him in the flowerbed. Across the street from the Jewish Agency." Nurit hesitates. Efrat can see her brain considering how much information to reveal to the vulnerable, pitiable fiancée.

"Yes?" Efrat urges. She wants to know everything.

Nurit stands up and puts her arm on Efrat's shoulder. "It's a miracle he's alive, you know."

"*Ness min ha'Shamyaim*," Nurit is saying, a miracle from God.

Is this the worst? Efrat wonders.

"He was badly burned . . . that is . . . charred," Nurit says.

Ah, she has saved the burns for last. "Mighty Grill," she mutters.

"Excuse me?" Nurit says.

"That's why he was on the bus. He went to change the damn lox." Efrat starts to cry, slowly at first, then sobs that overtake her body. She's tossing in her chair, a symphony of sobs. She wants to climb out of her skin, leave it here, her scarred, unmarried skin, and run away from the nightmare.

Nurit locks the door to the room. She helps Efrat stand up and hugs her. "It's OK, sweetheart," she says. "Cry."

When Efrat calms down, she wipes her eyes with the tissue and puts it back in her purse. Nurit takes her by the hand and leads her to the end of the long corridor, down the aisle, beds on either side. Nurit slides open the last curtain on the right. A white sheet covers a body. At the top of the body is a head, bandaged in gauze. Small holes for the eyes, nostrils, and mouth. Oren's lips are gray. Even the ears are covered in gauze, like a mummy.

Oren's eyes are closed, the brown eyes that promised *No more will you be lonely*, the eyes that held her with both mystery and familiarity, the eyes that assured, *Ha'kol yehiyeh b'seder, everything will be fine. We will marry on a Tuesday and build a home in Jerusalem and have children who love numbers and frogs.*

Efrat leans against Nurit for support.

An IV with menacing red and yellow lights sends out tubes that invade the body through the gauze dressing under the white sheet. A bag half full of urine the color of lemon juice hangs next to the bed. From the bag extends a clear plastic tube. Efrat does not want to imagine where it ends. He is a living mummy wrapped for burial. This is luck?

Slowly, Efrat walks to the chart hanging from the metal railing at the end of Oren's bed. She fingers the chart as if it too might ache from touch. She doesn't know what information she needs. Where are his clothes, his plaid socks that he wore when he left her this morning? Nurit brings her an orange plastic chair and places it next to the bed gently, as if a bang might kill.

"Sit," she whispers. "I'll bring you something to drink."

Efrat sits and again the tears dampen her cheeks. She wants her tears to form a river into which she can escape all this. She wants to float to a place where Tuesdays are always very good, as promised in Genesis. She opens her purse and takes out the damp tissue and wipes her eyes. Then she stands up and bends over Oren.

"I love you," she says, her words so light and soft they hardly move through the thick hospital air. "I do." She searches the eyes for a blink, prays for a quiver, but sees nothing. The eyelids sit like marble on Oren's still eyes.

A nurse comes by and checks the IV.

Efrat touches her arm. "We're getting married on Tuesday. *Pa'amayim ki tov.*" A *very* good day.

The next morning when Efrat awakes, her bed is damp with blood and tears. She goes to the bathroom to put in a tampon, turns on the classical music station, and thanks her walls for the four hours of dreamless sleep. On a piece of notepaper, she makes a list of all the people she has to call before she goes to the hospital and the airport. Dan at Mighty Grill, Bustan Abu Ghosh, the photographer, the florist, the DJ, and ah, yes, Micha the rabbi. Doda Viv!

Efrat hasn't seen her father for nine months. He comes home for ten weeks every nine months so he won't lose his health and pension rights at the National Insurance Institute. This morning she envies her father's ability to cut himself off from Israel.

At six thirty Efrat calls her mother in Tel Aviv, who complains she hasn't slept all night. Efrat coolly asks her to call the rabbi, DJ, and Mighty Grill. She gives her the numbers and hangs up. She calls Doda Viv and asks that she call Bustan Abu Ghosh, the photographer, and the florist to cancel and gives her the numbers. She wants to rush to the hospital so she will be there when Oren opens his eyes.

Efrat arrives at nine. Nurit explains to her that doctors frequently keep bomb victims in a drug-induced coma to help stabilize them.

"At least his condition did not worsen during the night," she says, as if Efrat should be grateful.

Efrat leans over Oren's face and places her mouth next to his covered ear. "I am here for you, sweetheart. I love you." Nothing reacts. "Tomorrow is our big day."

At the airport her father's plane has been delayed for an hour. Arrival time: 13:20. Efrat buys a double espresso and a croissant at the cafeteria. She sits and watches the sets of people coming into and leaving the waiting area and fantasizes about the family life of each group. She is so full of conflicting emotions that she bursts out crying when her father finally arrives. For the first thirty seconds he is aghast and holds her in his arms. She spills out everything between sobs.

When she calms down, he looks for the closest pay phone to call Thailand.

In the car on the way up to Jerusalem he talks about a new business deal, a hummus restaurant in a small village south of Bangkok. "This could be the next big thing, Frati," he says, explaining that Israeli tourists are starting to discover Thailand. "Would you like to come work for me?"

Efrat glances at her father, while keeping one eye on the road. Maybe he takes drugs. When did he become so out of touch? Was he always this way?

He doesn't kiss her when she lets him off at the Kings Hotel but rather pats her on the head as if she were some lost child. He has said nothing about the wedding or about Oren during the hour's drive from the airport to Jerusalem. She brushes off his hand and shuts the door behind him. He knocks on the window, begging to tell her something. She lowers it.

"Let me know how that man of yours is feeling," he says, swinging his bag over his shoulder, as if he's forgotten Oren's name. "I could use a man who's good with numbers."

Home by five, she collapses onto the couch, her head on the Indian pillow, and listens to messages. There are thirty-seven, but after the ninth she turns off the machine and, uncharacteristically, turns on the TV news. Now that she has seen Oren, nothing can shock her. The terrorist has been identified. Mustafa something, aged nineteen, a member of a small Hamas cell from Bethlehem. His accomplices videoed him before he left on his suicide mission, says the newscaster.

In the televised video, Mustafa is dancing at a cousin's wedding in Beit Jala. When the camera focuses on the bride and groom, Efrat covers her face with the Indian pillow. The bride's dress has the same French eyelet.

She bolts and calls Tanya. The line is busy, so she grabs her purse and runs out, down three flights of stairs, up Levi, a right at the corner, across Yehuda, up three flights of *shikun* stairs to Tanya's apartment. How could she forget? How could she forget?

Breathless at the door, she stands guilty. The news is still on. She hears the weatherman delivering the forecast for tomorrow, Tuesday, her wedding day: hot during the day, cooling slightly at night, especially in the mountainous regions. She rings the door-bell. Tanya opens the door, tilts her head to one side, and stares. Efrat doesn't know what to do. Tanya crosses her arms over her chest and stares more. When she speaks, finally, she says in a soft voice, "*Nu?* . . . I sew this beautiful dress, a dress for angels, lace from France, silk from Italy. Everyone sees. They ask, 'Who is this lucky bride? Who is this lucky bride?' Everyone wants touch dress, but I protect dress. 'No touch,' I say. 'Monday at three o'clock, you come see bride.' Two customers come. We wait, but angel no come. Not even call. *Nada.*"

Efrat doesn't know what to say, so she just stands there in the hallway.

"You couldn't call?"

Efrat leans against the doorway and stares into Tanya's eyes.

She wants Tanya to know without her having to tell. Tanya opens her arms and Efrat sinks into them. Her body begins to shake. Then she begins to sob. Tanya closes the door and leads Efrat into the fitting room.

"You didn't hear?" Efrat says, between sobs.

"I hear only sewing machine."

"Oren was wounded on the number 21."

Tanya holds Efrat in a hug. Efrat doesn't want her to let go. Tanya's soft flabby arms contain her sorrow, exhaustion, anger, despair, and fear. When she feels calm enough to speak, Efrat says, "He's in a coma. Deeply burned." She sniffles and looks for a tissue. Tanya pulls one from her pocket. "The nurse says I'm lucky."

Slowly Tanya releases Efrat and leads her to a chair.

"They say wait and see, *Savlanut*," Efrat says, "the magic words."

"The bastards," Tanya says.

Efrat buries her face in her hands and after a few minutes of silence asks to see her dress. Tanya walks over to the wall closet, slides open a door, and removes the hanger with the dress on it. It is covered with the floor-length plastic bag. "I protect dress," Tanya says, as she begins to slip off the bag.

Efrat stares and the staring improves her mood. "It's so beautiful," she says, "too beautiful to leave this room."

"No," says Tanya. "Take the dress. Try it on."

Efrat touches the dress, first with one finger, then with her whole hand. Her fingers caress the French eyelet bodice, the Italian silk skirt, the Spanish chiffon sleeves. She has never touched a newborn baby but imagines how one would with this heightened sense of delicacy.

She loves her dress. It is the embodiment of perfection, of the world she and Oren planned to build together. At the same moment, she also understands that it is no longer her wedding dress. It is the shroud of their wedding, the dress of her wound.

"I can't, Tanya."

"Take, take," Tanya insists. She covers up the dress with the plastic bag and drapes it over Efrat's arm. "It's yours."

"I'll call you," Efrat promises, already fearing she will forget again.

She leaves the apartment and walks slowly down the three flights of stairs, thinking each movement of her legs a blessing, each meeting place of skin with air a miracle. She walks slowly and if any of the shopkeepers on Bethlehem Road comment, she doesn't hear them, for she is lost in her own circle of sorrow. In this circle a plan comes to fruition, down Bethlehem Road carrying her wedding dress over her arm like a wounded bird. When she reaches her car on Levi, she spreads the dress out on the back seat and drives to the hospital.

The sun is setting in the west and the sky is golden pink, that unique hue that devoted Jerusalemites, like Efrat, love. It makes them drunk with an illusion of immortality. Twenty minutes later she parks at Hadassah. Gently she places the dress over her left arm and locks the car door with her right hand. The security guard recognizes her and lets her into the ER with no questions. She walks down the hall to Oren's aisle. On the way she hears oohs and aahs but does not stop to explain. She closes the curtain around his bed with her right hand and, as she creates this private space for them, she thinks of the chuppah at Bustan Abu Ghosh, how they would be married at about this time tomorrow, the sun setting, sky closing into darkness while a star or two yearns to appear.

The saline drips its steady solution as Efrat slips off the plastic bag and lets it fall to the floor. Then she holds her dress with two hands and lifts it in front of her like an offering, her hands turned upward to heaven. With care, she places the dress on top of the sheet that is covering Oren. She makes sure the waist of the dress covers where she assumes his waist must be. He makes no sound. She sees his chest move. His eyes are closed. It is a light dress, all lace chiffon and silk. It will not hurt him, this dress for an angel.

After the dress is spread over Oren's sheet, Efrat moves to the other side and sits in the chair next to the IV. She watches him breathe her dress, as if it were floating on the surface of a calm sea. As she watches Oren, she begins to breathe in sync with him, inhaling when he inhales, exhaling as he exhales. She feels closer to him than ever before, as if they are one body, helping each other stay alive. She marvels at this calm, as if the terror attack struck somewhere else.

Now she knows for sure she wants to marry this man, not just for the unborn children but because he will never leave her. Oren is the one. She will not let go. She will wait and see, wait and see until he sees her waiting and he is well and walking and when he sees, he will never leave.

Meanwhile, she will leave her dress on top of him until he awakes.

An hour later when she leaves the hospital and walks to her car, Efrat stops to look up at the night canopy. A dark silence covers her, punctured by a few stars. She hopes the angels on high are celebrating with her.

Train Crossing, Bethlehem Road
Meet Your Neighbor

Yehiel the Train Guy

I played with toy trains in Holland before the war so when the lady at the unemployment office offered me this job to raise and lower the barrier, I was delighted. OK, these aren't wooden trains and it's not my parents' living room, but still, lowering and raising the gate on Bethlehem Road, it reminds me of the days when the family was together, especially on the holidays when my cousins would come to Amsterdam from Utrecht and we'd take over the whole floor to build a train like the one that went all around Holland. My wife she says how can you sit there all day and do nothing. She never wants to see another train in her life, after Westerbork. What she doesn't know is that between trains I read books about trains, their history, how they're built, how much they cost. I read how they changed Europe and America and now I'm reading about the first train that came up to Jerusalem from Jaffa in 1895. Did you know Herzl's first train ride to Jerusalem took eleven and a half hours? Poor guy.

Imagine. We all walked places and then we used bicycles, especially in Holland, and then one day you go to the other side of the continent on a train! It's a miracle. Sometimes on Shabbat I sit on the floor at home and play with a caboose and pretend I'm in my parents' home and the war hasn't started yet.

THE FIRST PREGNANCY
IN JERUSALEM

... to be reborn into ... motherhood.
—Graffiti on a cave wall near Bethlehem

Even though the fetus was small enough to dance on the head of a pin, Helen Mor-Haim wanted to make sure it felt welcomed. She placed both hands on her bare skin below the navel and rubbed, one hand clockwise, the other counterclockwise. Surely the newbie would respond. But just in case, she asked David to kiss her symphysis pubis.

"Your what?" He lowered the volume of the 8:00 a.m. news.

"Big storm coming." She pointed to her abdomen and he leaned over to kiss. "Somewhere around here, right?"

After the kiss, Helen slithered out of bed and draped her tent dress over her head. She and David had chosen the gown the day after they had received the good news from the lab. More like a cloak of many colors, the dress vibrated with two-inch diagonal stripes of red, yellow, orange, and green. She knew it made her look like a clown, but she didn't care. She wanted everyone in Jerusalem to know that after four years of taking her temperature every morning, three years of taking Clomiphene to jump-start her ovulation, two years of praying, and lots of mechanical fucking, Helen Mor-Haim was with child. She wanted the whole city—east and west, Arabs, Christians, and Jews, believers and skeptics alike—to rejoice, because finally, unto Helen and David, *tfu tfu*, a child would be born in Jerusalem.

David kissed her again, this time on the lips. "Home by six," he said.

"It's in your hands," said Helen, tickling his ears.

"What is?"

"Time," Helen said.

Alone in the house with only her unborn child, not yet even a fish, Helen walked to the kitchen and squeezed two oranges. Then she toasted a bagel. Everything, since receiving the good news from the lab, reminded her of birth. Her juices would break at the end of the ninth; the baby would slip down the bagel hole of her vaginal canal. She couldn't look at milk without thinking, *Baby*.

"You're going to be a mother," she told the image in the bathroom mirror, while combing her hair. Would he have her straight brown or David's black curly?

At 9:00 a.m. Helen put on her purple rain jacket, accentuating the clownish effect. Now she was an all-weather walking circus tent. She slipped on her magenta backpack and walked out the door. As she turned around to lock, she wondered what she had forgotten. Ever since conception, or what she called "takeoff," Helen had begun to forget things—her daily apple, her identity card. David said it was hormones playing havoc with the time zones in her brain. But now it was time to take off for work, apple or no apple.

The crisp February air pinched Helen's face. She unlatched

the iron gate and turned toward the train tracks, as she had done every day for the past three years. She and David had purchased the large one-story Arab house at 64 Bethlehem Road in 1967 with the help of both their parents. They fell in love with the jasmine bush in front and the garden behind the house the first time they saw it. They imagined five unborn Mor-Haims swinging from the branches of the mulberry tree, but as each barren year passed, they realized one healthy child would be a blessing.

Helen smelled the coming rain. It sweetened the air, despite the fumes from the number 6 bus. She walked by the taciturn art professor's home at 62, the man who never said hello. Rumor had it that his wife left him one night, carrying their baby in her arms. The artist had thrown an easel at her when he was drunk. Helen never saw his paintings, all variations, according to rumor, on the Madonna and child.

In front of the two-story house at 56 Bethlehem Road, corner of Shimshon, Helen stopped to look at the trees in the yard. Branches of the fig and pomegranate were gray and bare. Silver leaves at the crest of the olive tree rustled in the wind. Only the almond tree blossomed, its delicate white flowers conjuring rows of soft, clean diapers.

Helen felt a gurgling in her stomach. The gurgling rose to her chest, then her throat. Before she knew what was happening, she was leaning over the low stone wall encircling the yard and retching onto the roots of the olive tree. She cupped her abdomen, fearing the force of her retch might dislodge the fetus. What if it came out of her nose? An orangey-yellow-green bile, dotted with pieces of toasted bagel, formed a puddle at the roots of the tree. She lowered her backpack to the sidewalk and took out a tissue to wipe her mouth.

In her five books on pregnancy, Helen had read about morning sickness, but this was her first experience. Though it left a sour taste in her mouth, she knew it was a good sign. Now she could officially count herself among the order of pregnant women. She began to walk again, looking around to see if anyone had seen her. Simcha, wrapped in an orange knitted shawl, sat in her open door at number 54, fishing for stones in brown lentils. At 52 Bethlehem Road, two women, old enough to be great-grandmothers, waited for a cab in front of Beit Avraham Retirement Home. Helen was hurt nobody noticed her pregnancy dress, especially on a street where everyone knew everyone else's business.

At the railroad crossing, Helen waved to Yehiel, sitting in his brick hut, waiting for the 9:09. She pointed to her stomach.

What gives? he asked by raising his hand over his head and twisting it at the wrist.

"I'm pregnant," she yelled from the other side of Bethlehem Road.

"It's about time," he shouted. "If it's a boy, I come to the *brit*."

"What about the trains?"

"We can do the *brit* here!" he shouted.

Helen laughed and hoped laughter would not dislodge her progeny. Yehiel loudly hummed a phrase from the chorus of Handel's *Messiah*.

Of course her miniscule angel was a boy.

As she crossed the tracks into the German Colony and waved goodbye to Yehiel, she floated into another time zone. The large stone building that served as a hospice, church, girls' school, and convent of the Borromean nuns, along with the two-story stone homes with their gabled roofs, small vegetable patches, and low stone walls, catapulted Helen to the world of nineteenth-century messianic Germans. German Templers came to this part of Jerusalem to hasten the coming of the Messiah. For Helen, walking to work every day was moving from Baka, a mid-twentieth-century immigrant neighborhood, to a nineteenth-century neighborhood built by Germans. Helen loved crossing time zones with her feet.

She held her nose as she walked past the Hadar cookie factory. Usually she enjoyed the smells escaping from the open front doors, but not today. At number 14, people were going in and out of the mental health clinic. She wondered what went on there, if it was truly a place for healing or a stopgap that pushed pills. Everyone had a story in Israel, but which ones caused people to go over the edge? She crossed the street at the Sonol station and walked on the side of Yemin Moshe. She always imagined the windmill moving, even though it had never moved since its construction a hundred years earlier. Dreamers, the city drew dreamers like a magnet.

Walking up King David Street, Helen encountered the first drops of rain. The YMCA on her left glistened in the morning drizzle. Its bell tower looked more like a cervix than a phallus this morning. She checked her watch: seven minutes late.

Mr. Shlomo Ben-David gave her a nasty look as she took off her damp jacket and backpack and staked her position behind the counter.

"Sorry," she said, erasing dust from the counter with her forearm.

"I thought Americans respect time, Helen. That is why I hired you."

"I'm Canadian, Mr. Ben-David, and you hired me because of my degree." Helen knew she was wasting her BA in Byzantine history by selling authentic and fake artifacts to tourists. "I'm pregnant, remember? I told you on Friday." Helen put her hands on her belly. "I was detained," she said, with self-righteous drama. The bitter taste still filled her mouth.

She walked to the bathroom to drink some water. When she caught a glimpse of herself in the mirror, the tilt of her head reminded her of one of the Mary statues on the top shelf. She chuckled, imagining an olive wood statue of the Virgin Mary, with morning sickness.

"Hear the news this morning?" Ben-David picked up a feather duster to spruce up the near-life-size olive wood crèche in the entrance of the store.

"No," Helen said, behind her counter. "What miracle happened this morning in the City of Peace?" Helen vowed not to listen to the news during pregnancy, so the tensions in the country would not affect her child. Why start life with fear and trembling, if you could start with love and peace? She had enough fears about her pregnancy and birth without the daily explosions. Would she make it to term? Would she survive birth? Would the baby be whole?

"You remember the crazy tourist who set fire to El Aksa in August? They send him home today."

"Good riddance," Helen said. "Let the Aussies deal with him."

"He says on the news he set fire so we can rebuild the Temple . . ."

"Right."

". . . to bring the Second Coming."

"Sure."

". . . to save the world."

Helen put her hands on her heart to calm its beat. "Another messianic *meshuganeh*."

Mr. Ben-David spit on Joseph's head to get rid of an especially stubborn piece of dirt. He moved Joseph closer to Mary and turned them both to face the door.

"David says it's called the Jerusalem Syndrome," Helen said.

"What?"

"People coming to Jerusalem and going crazy." She looked at the coin under the glass counter with the large pomegranate embossed on it and thought of her unborn son. Would he be an economist or a king?

Mr. Ben-David turned the olive wood crib between Joseph and Mary to face the door as well. Helen thought the three statues she stared at daily and tried to sell to pilgrims were nothing more than figures of a simple family in bathrobes, adoring their new baby. She wondered why every pilgrim who entered the store had to touch them with their greasy hands, move them, make such a to-do. Didn't every new family look alike?

At 10:10 a.m., Uri from Egged Tours brought in a group of fifteen evangelicals. "Good morning, Shlomo," he said to Ben-David and nodded to Helen. In Hebrew he added, "From this group I want 15 percent, not the usual 10."

Ben-David turned to the pilgrims. "Welcome, welcome. We have beautiful olive wood carvings of the holy family, original Roman coins, Byzantine oil lamps. Please, come in. Make yourselves at home."

A smile automatically covered Helen's face as she spread her arms over her goods. She could sell oil lamps to electricians.

All during February and March, on her way to work, Helen Mor-Haim retched onto the roots of the same olive tree.

The almond blossoms gave way to tender green almonds. In April dainty buds, the color of mother's milk, opened on the olive tree. The leaves of the fig stretched their five perfect fingers. Everything grew, along with Helen's fetus.

One morning, Helen was beside what she now called "my olive tree." After wiping her mouth, she looked up and saw two pregnant women riding toward her, sitting sidesaddle on two gray asses. They were being led by two men holding twine cords tied around the asses' necks. Every few seconds one of the men glanced over his shoulder to see if his wife—Helen assumed the couples were married—was still there. The men slouched toward Bethlehem.

When the couples stopped in front of Helen, she saw idols in a sack hanging from the ass on the left. She understood the woman was Rachel, the man Jacob. The other woman had an enormous bosom. Her eyes focused on some rustic birthing site beyond Baka. Her husband carried two two-by-fours strapped to his back. Helen recognized Mary and Joseph.

Like acorns, the belly buttons of both women bulged from under their brown linen robes. Their eyes focused on the clear sky above. Helen assumed the women were ripe to give birth. After they passed Helen, Rachel turned back and winked.

Helen was shocked. How could Rachel and Mary ride asses during Braxton-Hicks contractions? She stood immobile by the low stone wall and stared at her olive tree. Its trunk, contorted like snakes, reminded her of biblical signs and wonders.

That night, while David washed dishes, Helen lost herself in rumination. The morning ritual of vomiting on the roots of the same olive tree, what did it mean? The vision, why her? She approached the kitchen sink and put her arms around David's waist.

"Mmm," he purred. "More."

She pressed her head into his back. He balanced his hands on the marble counter and let the water run.

"Something big is happening, David."

"I know, sweetheart. Only six more months. Or is it five?"

"No. Something bigger."

David turned off the water and turned around. He put his hands on Helen's belly.

"What's bigger than this?"

"Promise you won't laugh?"

"Promise."

"I had a sign."

"A sign?"

"I've discovered the birth sites of Benjamin and Jesus."

David leaned back against the counter, lowered his arms, then placed the palm of his hand on Helen's forehead. "Let's sit, sweetheart." He led her to the couch.

"It's right here, David, on Bethlehem Road." Her speech sounded dreamy. "You know the garden on the corner of Shimshon?"

"The neglected yard?"

"I vomit there every morning, always on the roots of the same olive tree."

"So?"

"It's a sign, David. Don't you see?"

David ran his hand through his hair. "No, I don't see, Helen." He shook his head in silence.

"Only a pregnant woman could discover this holy site."

He looked at her with a combination of love and concern.

"The traditional birthplace of Benjamin is ambiguous," Helen said. "And Jesus? Helena determined his birthplace more than three hundred years after his birth. All she had to go on was a grotto."

David stared into his wife's brown eyes. Helen could tell he was thinking, *Hormones*.

"Destiny, David, not hormones; destiny has me puke on those roots."

"Who's Helena?"

"The queen, Constantine's mother." Helen gasped. "Oh my God, David. Another sign. Helena. I never . . ."

David gathered his lower lip with his top teeth.

"If we dig where I puke every day," Helen continued, "we'll find a grotto full of shards. I'm sure, David. We'll smell myrrh, right here, on our street. This is big, David, big."

David took a pillow from the end of the couch, folded it in half, and stuck it behind his back.

"We'll find the jawbones of two asses, for Christ's sake," Helen said, raising her voice.

He touched her lips with his forefinger.

"We'll find the letters RHL and MRM carved in charcoal on the walls of the grotto," she whispered. "I had a vision."

"A vision? . . . As in television?"

"Stop it, David. This is serious."

"You're right, honey."

"Our son will be a savior, David." Helen put her head on David's chest, her heart racing from the idea of exposing a new piece of holy ground and giving birth to a savior. Jerusalem flaunted innumerable holy sites, but it took a pregnant woman named Helen to reveal one in the twentieth century.

"Are you tired?" David asked, yawning.

"If it's not their birth sites, it could be their mothers' burial sites. I saw Rachel and Mary there this morning."

For the next month, every morning on her way to work, Helen stopped to look at the olive tree whose roots reached her past and future. Every day, while staring at her tree, she fantasized the glory that would envelop her after the Israel Antiquities Authority confirmed her theory. David had suggested calling them after the birth, rather than during the pregnancy; she agreed.

On May 5, in her fifth month, while standing by the low stone wall, Helen felt a force pulling her right side toward work. A counter force tugged at her left side. She stretched both arms and allowed herself to be pulled in opposite directions. Ben-David could get along without her today. She lowered her right arm and allowed her left to point the way.

To her surprise, she walked past her home and kept walking—past Doda Rosa's candy shack, past Igor the butcher, past Falafel Ovadia, and past Menachem's bakery. At Weissman's Furniture, where Baka became semi-industrial, she imagined buying a soft, rotund couch that would host her new family of three. Three? Maybe she had more than one. Didn't Tamar walk around rubbing her stomach, saying, "I will give birth to saviors and kings"? The thought made Helen's head spin. What about Rivka? Oy.

At the end of Bethlehem Road, the invisible force continued to pull south. Helen walked up to Hebron Road and turned right toward Bethlehem. The urban landscape opened into well-tended olive groves and vineyards. On a hillock to her right, she passed the Egyptian plane shot down during the Six-Day War. How close it had come to bombing her. How lucky she was to be alive, a child growing inside her, who would one day save . . . What would he save?

She walked past the Monastery of Mar Elias and imagined another church, an early Byzantine church that stood somewhere along this road. Surely, before the end of the millennium, an archaeologist would find it, the place that marked Mary's route to Bethlehem. One day they would build a gas station there. All holy sites in Israel were blessed with gas stations.

Would opening her secret grotto to tourists turn Bethlehem Road into an unbearable traffic jam? While half of her mind contemplated this possibility, the other half wondered why she couldn't concentrate on her mother's questions: *Which diaper service? Will you nurse? Planning to go back to work?* The landscape invited her to a distant, romantic past that towered mythic in her imagination, though her belly protruded into the future.

Beyond Tantur Ecumenical Institute, Helen came to a small booth manned by two Israeli soldiers.

"I'm pregnant," she said, straightening her striped circus tent over her belly. She bestowed a beatific smile.

The soldiers looked at each other and snickered.

"Mazal tov," one said. His eyes gleamed under his red hair. King David.

"So?" the other one asked.

"So, an invisible force is pulling me to Bethlehem."

The less handsome soldier pointed to his head and winked at his comrade.

"Let me check your ID card and your backpack," King David said.

Helen took off her pack and opened it. She rummaged for her ID. "It must be at home," she said.

The soldiers conferred, checked her backpack, and let her pass.

"Next time, bring your ID," King David shouted behind her.

After the crossing, the scenery changed. Modest stone stores selling bamboo furniture, olive wood rosaries, and fresh fruits and vegetables lined the main road, which didn't have sidewalks. Outside Rachel's Tomb, religious Jewish women gathered, their eyes still wet from their prayers for a son, or even a daughter. At Manger Square, hundreds of tourists milled around haggling with vendors selling wooden crosses and rosary beads. The braying of donkeys and the buzz of foreign languages enveloped her. She saw Uri from Egged Tours leading his group into the Manger Meat Restaurant, but she looked the other way. She did not want questions.

The invisible force pulled her to the Church of the Nativity. At the low entrance, she held her belly with both hands, knelt, and walked in. Inside reigned a celestial smell and silence. Helen took a few deep breaths, as deep as possible with the baby taking up so much space. The enormous Crusader pillars awed her, as did the majesty of the basilica. She was moved toward the stairs to the right of the altar, where several nuns knelt in front of candles, holding their hands in prayer. The narrow, twisted stone staircase pulled her to the grotto, where silver lamps dangled from a dark ceiling. Nobody was there. Incense emanating from the walls of the grotto made her dizzy. She faced the low iron grate, behind which, embedded in white marble, exploded the fourteen-pointed silver star. This was the place, the exact place, according to Queen Helena, where the Jewish boy who became Jesus was born.

Helen's baby kicked.

〜⌒〜

How did Sarah, Rachel, Hannah, and Mary give birth without breathing lessons? This question bothered Helen when, in June, during her sixth month, she saw an ad on a telephone pole that promised "A Birth without Screaming." In small print she read: "You are in control, supported by a trained husband or friend." When she dialed Elisabeth, the Lamaze teacher, to confirm her first meeting, Helen almost fainted when Elisabeth revealed her address: 7 Our Matriarch Rachel Street.

David was glad Helen was focusing on the present. He looked forward to sharing the classes. On July 1 at 8:30 p.m., they were the first couple to arrive at Elisabeth's home. Elisabeth was a tall, slender woman who had one son. She wore a purple gown with a hooded mantle and sprayed the room with matronly smiles.

By 8:40 Helen was astonished to see five other women as pregnant as she. For six months she had thought she was the only pregnant woman in Jerusalem, so absorbed was she in her inner life. Now, here were couples like David and her, all expecting their first child. They dampened her spirits.

"We can do this on our own," she whispered in David's sensitive ear before Elisabeth began.

"Let's hear her," he said. She could tell he was annoyed. He started talking basketball to another first-time father, who, like himself, sat on the floor at his wife's feet.

Elisabeth knelt in front of the group and held up a three-by-two-foot illustrated poster of the inner world. Shades of orange and brown dominated. With her right index finger, Elisabeth charted the fetus's course down through the cervix, into the birth canal, and out the vagina.

David turned to his wife. "Fabulous, isn't it, honey? Reminds me of Magellan."

"It's banal, David. Let's go home."

The other couples motioned them to be quiet.

Why didn't anyone teach the mythic side of pregnancy?

"You can control your contractions," Elisabeth said with a passive aggression that made Helen want to vomit. "Just breathe."

Helen put her hands over her belly to protect her son's ears from nonsense.

"Husbands, you are here to support. Prop up her pillows. Make sure her focal point doesn't fall off the wall. Wipe the sweat from her brow."

Helen poked David with her knee. "This is bullshit," she whispered.

"It's important, honey," he said, turning to her. "There's no reason to be scared."

"Who's scared?"

In three months she would give birth to a savior. Maybe he would become a prince or a king. She didn't know what might happen, but she knew the miracles of pregnancy and birth were so much more exciting than Elisabeth's little trip down the canal.

By the end of July, David was reading Helen's books on pregnancy. She had switched to *The Book of Psalms*.

In August, her eighth month, Helen quit working for Ben-David. She could not look at another olive wood carving of Jesus nor a coin of the Virgin Mary. Besides, she had work to do. She and her savior son needed an indoor biblical landscape. It was time to decorate the empty beige room. Her mother had sent eight rolls of sanitized wallpaper from Toronto—a crisp snow-white background scattered with bombastic orange, yellow, and red flowers. Not exactly biblical but definitely washable.

One night, while David was watching the news, Helen climbed a wooden ladder to cover the boring walls with paste. She thanked God when she got down safely. Then David came, climbed the ladder, and spread the sheets of Sanitas wallpaper. Within three hours, the depressing walls of the baby's room exuded the smell of a sanitized Garden of Eden.

"I'll buy a blue carpet," Helen said, "the color of living waters. This will be our *umbilicus mundi.*" David gave her a look. It was the look he had been giving her since she returned from the Grotto of the Nativity. It said: *You're not giving birth to a savior.*

"Then I'll buy an acacia table and one of those lamps shaped like Noah's ark."

David walked into the bathroom.

"I want a lampshade with biblical scenes," she continued, louder.

David shouted from the bathroom, "How about the Sacrifice of Isaac?"

During the middle of the ninth month, Braxton-Hicks contractions came often. They were like ocean waves that started simultaneously on both sides of the full-blown circus tent and crashed in the middle. All Helen had to do was breathe deeply, count, and pretend she was riding a wave. Toward the end of September, however, contractions became stronger. One night while Helen was chanting Psalm 91 and the TV blared inflation, contractions came every three minutes.

"Big storm coming," she said to David.

"Finally, good news."

They drove to the hospital.

At the reception desk, she told the lady that she was either giving birth to the Messiah or she would die in childbirth. The midwife who accepted them looked at David to see if he, too, was unbalanced.

Helen shook David's arm. "Look at her badge. Shifra!"

"So what?" David said. "Grab hold of yourself." Raising his voice above the hospital din, he reminded Helen that Elisabeth said to report the *frequency* of the contractions, not the *outcome* of the birth. Then he turned to Shifra. "I don't know what happened to her. She was fine when we left home, but on the way she forgot how to breathe."

Shifra wrote down everything.

Helen noticed the long black hands of the clock on the wall. They reminded her of forceps stretching beyond the clock's green plastic frame. It was ten after seven in the evening, September 27, 1970, two days before Rosh Hashana, the creation of the world. Helen knew that Rosh Hashana was also the new year for kings and felt sure this was another sign that her son would be a regal savior.

The hands of the clock embraced Helen. She tried to relax.

"How many do you have in there?" Shifra asked, directing Helen to the scale and patting her stomach. Throughout the pregnancy Helen had eaten whatever torte she encountered. Her favorite was the Esterhazy. Hidden in the circus-tent robe, her extra weight would never show. Now some nasty midwife was mistaking a few pieces of scrumptious Hungarian delights for another fetus. "Yocheved gave birth to a myriad, you know."

"Why this midrashic humor?" Helen retorted. "Isn't it bad enough that I will be sainted or dead within twenty-four hours?"

"Take her up to X-ray on the eighth floor," Shifra commanded David.

The X-ray showed one big fetus.

Back on the ground floor, Shifra grabbed Helen's arm and walked her to a bed in a labor room. David followed and taped a poster of the Temple Mount on the wall opposite. She had chosen the Dome of the Rock for her focal point. It covered Adam, Abraham, and Mohammed, all of humanity, maybe, rising, as it did, over the Foundation Stone of the world, the site closest to heaven, from which all light first shone on pregnant women. From the abyss under the Foundation Stone an underground spring watered the world. Surely the waters that would break between her legs any minute would spring directly from that source.

All night Helen sucked strawberry lollipops for energy while David dozed on the fake leather chair next to her bed. A doctor with a one-syllabic name periodically came into the room, snickered at Helen's focal point, and checked the dilation.

"I'm afraid we'll have to give you Pitocin, young lady," the doctor said in the morning.

"It's another sign," Helen said softly.

"Sign?" the doctor said.

"Like Moses and Jeremiah, my son is reluctant."

The doctor turned to see if a nurse was available. "Pitocin stimulates contractions," he said, as if he had invented it.

Helen spent the day drugged. She treaded through contractions in liminal time. The doctor had snuck in some Valium with the

Pitocin, which created a fog not conducive to Lamaze. David roamed the ward. When he took up position next to Helen, he lifted the damp washcloth hanging over the bed railing and wiped his own forehead.

"This isn't anything like Elisabeth's course," he complained.

As if God had waited for the evening shift, at exactly 6:05 p.m. on September 28, Helen experienced long, hard contractions every ninety seconds.

"Ask someone if this is transition," she told David. By the time he returned, the dome had ditched the rock.

"This hurts," Helen yelled. David scurried around looking for a doctor. Helen screamed, "I want to push."

To Helen this was a sign that, like Eve, she would give birth in pain.

No sooner had she thought of Eve than she heard a voice say, "You can't push yet." A tall nurse with long black hair appeared beside her. "We're taking you to the delivery room now."

Was this Lilith, Adam's first wife?

In the delivery room another woman in white, this one with henna hair and hot-pink nails, entered, holding a large injection. Helen assumed it was for the woman at the end of the room screaming, "Save me, *emaleh*." When she put the needle in Helen's arm, Helen was convinced she had chosen the wrong hospital.

"This will quiet you down," said the nurse.

"I don't want to be quiet," Helen shouted. "I want to shriek and push. I want to shit a watermelon."

The black hands of the clock on the wall again stretched beyond the green frame to embrace Helen, who was angry at her unborn son. Would he always be late?

The devil doctor approached. He stood near Helen's left

shoulder, towering above her, on his lips a snicker. "So how is your Lamaze breathing?" he chortled.

A red tie hung around his neck beneath his white doctor's coat. Helen vowed to strangle him if she survived the birth.

David stood opposite the doctor. He too wore a white coat, but he resembled a lost Bedouin. When his cheeks turned white as well, Lilith suggested he take a seat against the wall.

"We can handle this," she assured him.

He sat down and covered his face, leaning against the white wall. The devil doctor lifted his two giant hands and let them fall on Helen's belly. Then he pushed.

"He's mine," Helen screamed. "I'll push him out. He's mine."

This only made the devil push harder.

"Your baby doesn't want to come out," he said, "so we're going to have to help."

Helen saw his ugly hands in fists above her heart. With all his weight he leaned onto her belly. Helen tried to push him away, but he pushed her arms.

This is a test, she thought. Rachel and Mary were tested. Now God is asking me: "Whose baby is this, the devil's or yours?"

"He's mine, he's mine," Helen yelled. "Leave him alone."

The clock stopped. Helen inhaled like a wild boar.

"*Ahhhhhh!*" she shrieked, exhaling slowly.

Everyone in the delivery room stepped back from the delivery table. Then, in some miraculous way, for she had no strength left, Helen rose up. She huffed and puffed. She inhaled air and blew fire. She farted and shat. She sang hymns in English, Latin, and Greek. She recited psalms in Hebrew and French. She cursed the doctor in Arabic. He froze, then left. The entire medical staff was too scared to come near her.

"Surely, the power of the Lord is with her," they murmured.

"He's coming," she shouted. "Save me."

All this commotion woke David. He wiped his eyes and took up position where the little devil's head was emerging between Helen's legs.

"Big," David said, almost collapsing again. "This is big."

A squeak broke a sound barrier, shattering time. Pieces burst and dropped on everyone like rain.

At 7:56 p.m., the hands resumed their click.

On Rosh Hashana, the birthday of the world, Helen awoke in a hospital bed on the maternity ward. From the breakfast tray at the foot of her bed, she understood she had not died and gone to heaven. She took out a mirror from the top drawer of the metal nightstand next to her bed and held it to her face. Yellow lines crossed her cheeks like goat trails in the Judean wilderness. Brown and blue circles cupped her eyes. Was this the body from which a son had emerged with such signs and wonders? But . . . But . . . Where was the baby? Why did the midwives not bring him? Did Lilith kill all firstborn males?

A blonde nurse with the nametag that read "Anne" wheeled in a plastic basket. She squinted at the mother's name on the basket. "Helena?"

"No. Helen. That's me . . . the mother." No sooner had the m-word left her lips than Anne pushed the bundle toward her.

"Wait," said Helen, seeds of panic on her tongue. "What do I do?"

Anne set the package on Helen's knees. "Like so," she said in a Russian accent, lifting Helen's arms to accept a pillow. Anne then picked up the stuffed parcel and presented it. "Like so," she repeated, arranging Helen's left arm under the infant's head with the assurance of a general.

Keep breathing, Helen told herself.

The thing in the blanket wiggled and quivered. It had two glassy eyes the size of lentils, a nose that in some miraculous way knew how to channel air in and out, two ears that seemed to Helen more interesting than any Byzantine text, and a mouth that, when opened fully, revealed a damp, red abyss. No teeth. Pure lips twittered. His hair had not yet chosen brown or black. Hidden behind the creature's precarious skin, real organs pulsed. Helen felt them.

Anne helped Helen hook the baby onto her nipple. Then Helen draped a large white cotton diaper over herself and her son. They were alone together in the white grotto. Time melted. Helen felt hearts beat. He slurped; she heard the waves. The smell of his skin was sweet to her nostrils. She kissed his head.

David walked into the room. He lifted the white tent. Helen smiled through her tears. He kissed her right cheek and the baby's head.

"I forgot who I was," Helen said, in a voice she did not recognize. "Now, we're three."

When the baby let go of the nipple, Helen placed him against her bent knees. David stared, then circled the bed to view the mother and child from all angles, biting his lip.

Helen looked into David's eyes and remembered loving, that feeling when time burst like the Red Sea and they floated into a good, new place where all clocks stopped and calendars lost their meaning.

"You're back," he said, stroking her hair. "Present tense."

Helen smiled. She rubbed their baby's belly. "He saved me . . . us . . ."

"From what?"

"From . . ." She wasn't sure how to phrase it, but then the ancient word appeared: ". . . barrenness."

She watched her son's lips rest in peace. Inside, where nobody could see, she felt a profound width and depth, a space with no borders, a place large as the sky and at the same time small as the head of a pin, a place so close to creation she could feel it with every breath. She would always watch her baby's arms, fingers, legs, toes, mouth, nose, and eyes. She would never stop marveling at the miracle of his intricate ears. Nothing—neither history nor God, neither devil nor Bible, not even the holy geography of Jerusalem—would pull her out of the present.

Uri the Egged Tour Guide

Thank you for joining me on our walking tour of Baka. We will end here on the corner of Bethlehem Road and Rivka. I hope you appreciate how the neighborhood has changed over the past ninety years, from a pastoral Arab neighborhood full of magnificent homes encircled by pomegranate, fig, and olive trees and fields for grazing sheep from the nearby Arab villages to a bustling multicultural city-burb.

We're proud of our sidewalks, stop signs, and buses. We love our falafel and Moshe's new copy machine. But mainly it's the wonderful people who have come from all over the world that makes Baka great. It is no coincidence that Ingathering of the Exiles Street is here.

If you want to continue walking south toward Bethlehem, note the archaeological site behind the gas station on your left. Mary stopped there on her way to give birth. On your right, don't miss the Jordanian plane we shot down in 1967. Further on, you'll see the Tantur Ecumenical Institute. They used to show a model of the olive tree on which Jesus was crucified, but due to the crossfire of Palestinian militants and the Israeli army last year, this model has been relocated to Ein Kerem, also a wonderful place to visit.

Be sure to tell your friends back home about Baka and come back soon. By the way, if any of you are thinking about relocating or immigrating to the area or are interested in investing, my wife just happens to be a real estate agent. Here is her card.

Find your home on Bethlehem Road with Mrs. Egged Turz, realtor.
02-5709741

FAMILY LIFE

. . . and you shall be comforted in Jerusalem.

ISAIAH 66:13

EVERY MAN A LAMB

On the Shabbat *Ki Tisa*, when the Jewish people lose their patience with Moses, build a golden calf, and the Levites murder three thousand stiff-necked Jews, Dr. Dick Coen, a newcomer to Baka, meets a neighbor as they reach for the same rugelach.

"Please, you first," says the man from the right side of the kiddush table.

"No, no," says Coen. "I just want a little something sweet for my kids." Amy and Joel cower behind their father, as they do every Shabbat when he drags them to one of the twenty-five neighborhood synagogues for kiddush.

"You drink the Golden Calf?"

Coen smiles. He has no idea what the man is talking about. He scoops a handful of Bamba for Joel and grabs an isolated rugelach for Amy, which she stuffs into her mouth whole.

"Moroccans," he whispers to the kids.

"Can we go home now?" asks Joel.

Coen feels a meaty tap on his shoulder. He turns around. The man is standing there, almost on top of him, his hand stretching toward Coen's chest. The first reaction is to push him away.

"Abutbul," says the man.

"Coen. Dr. Dick Coen," he says, taking two steps back, nearly trampling his kids. "We live over there." He points to the three-story building on Bethlehem Road diagonally across the street from Tikvatenu Synagogue. "Top floor."

"You come visit?"

Coen doesn't know if Abutbul is asking about an event in the past, present, or future.

"I slaughter morning of the Seder. Bring the kids. You surgeon, no?"

"Chiropractor," Coen says. The four syllables probably don't mean a thing to this man.

"Good," says Abutbul, "then you come."

Coen takes a sip of wine from the flimsy paper cup he has been holding in his left hand. "You're going to kill an animal in your house?" He hopes he is not speaking too loudly. Maybe all Moroccans do this. On the day before Yom Kippur he took Joel to the *shuk*. As they walked past a butcher shop, Joel screamed. The butcher was swinging a live chicken over a man's head. The chicken screeched and wailed as the butcher pulled the chicken's neck back and slit its throat with a knife. Joel's screaming got louder. Dick had to carry him out of the *shuk*, holding him close to his chest like a baby.

"On roof," Abutbul says, pointing to the roof of the house on the corner of Reuven and Bethlehem Road. "For Pesach. You know, Pesach sacrifice." Abutbul slaps both his thighs. "Our roots."

Roots. That's why he agreed to follow Bonnie to Jerusalem. Roots. The longer he lives here—not even a year yet—the stronger he feels about his roots in Boston.

"We slaughter. You watch," Abutbul says, chuckling. "Like in *beit knesset*. We pray. You eat."

Dick wonders if the man is brain-damaged or if it's just the language barrier. A scar on the lower left side of Abutbul's chin makes him think of Mafia movies. Dick squeezes the empty paper cup. Drops of red wine spurt onto Joel's white shirt.

"Of course," says Dick to Abutbul. "We'd love to."

"That's disgusting," Bonnie says when Dick tells her about the invitation. "You can't take the kids to a sacrifice." They're sitting around the table finishing their Shabbat lunch. "It's not even Jewish."

"Of course it's Jewish, Bon. It's Moroccan Jewish." Dick leaves the table to take down their Koren Bible from the top of the TV. "Exodus, chapter twelve, Abutbul told me. Says right here: *On the tenth day of this month they shall take to them every man a lamb* blah blah blah *and if the household be too little for the lamb*—like us—*let him and his neighbor next to his house*—like Abutbul—*take it* blah blah blah."

"His neighbor?" Bonnie says.

"I'm reading what's on the page, Bon. *Your lamb shall be without blemish, a male of the first year: you shall take it from the sheep or from the goats and you shall keep it until the fourteenth day of the same month . . .*"

"When's that?"

"How should I know? The month of Pesach, I guess . . . *and the whole assembly of the congregation of Israel shall kill it toward evening*. End of quote."

"That's disgusting," says Joel. "I'm not going to any killing." He turns toward his mother. "Mom, don't let him take me."

"Dick, nobody does the Pesach sacrifice since the Temple was destroyed. Rabbi Benstock said so."

"Benstock doesn't know Abutbul," says Dick.

"What? Our temple was destroyed? Why didn't you tell me?" Joel is up in arms about B'nai Avraham's demise. He loved their *hamantaschen.*

"No, Joel, the Holy Temple, the one that stood in Jerusalem two thousand years ago," says Bonnie. "B'nai Avraham is still in Newton."

"Nobody does the sacrifice from Boston, Bon. Abutbul and his Atlas Mountain clan have been sacrificing lambs since, I don't know, since before Paul Revere. Now they do it right across the street. You wanted roots? Here they are, right here on Bethlehem Road. I'm taking the kids to watch."

"I want to go to a Red Sox game," Joel says. Ever since the Coens' arrival in Israel, Joel has been scrounging candy stores for baseball cards. Doda Rosa across the street has never even heard of baseball cards. Joel can't understand how kids can grow up without them.

"I don't blame you, kid. I prefer the Red Sox to killing lambs," Dick says, "but when in Rome . . ."

Amy jumps off her chair. "Yippee. We're going to see the lamb!"

Dick sees Bonnie's body contract, as if she's been hit by a bat.

"Rabbi Benstock says only when the Temple gets rebuilt can we go back to sacrificing." She's talking into her plate of chicken and *kugel.* "That won't happen until the Messiah comes."

"You wait," Dick says. "On the morning of the Seder, I'm taking the kids across the street."

"Yippee," Amy repeats.

"There's enough blood in the news, Dick. Don't spoil our first Pesach here."

"You were the one dying to enter Jewish history, Bon. Right here we have a front-row seat. Christ, it's even better than that. We're on the frigging field."

Bonnie insists on the family singing grace after meals. Dick doesn't have the patience. He stands up and clears the table. He tells Joel to help him, but Joel instead pushes Amy onto the stone floor. She cries. Dick raises his hand with an empty water glass into first position, the one that says, *Do as you're told, or else.*

Bonnie sits at the table by herself, mouthing the words to the short version. After she finishes praying, she goes to the sink. Facing the dirty dishes, she says, "Don't touch the child."

Four days before the Seder, when Dick is sitting on the couch with Joel and Amy, looking out the living room window, enjoying the view of the new apartments rising in the Gilo neighborhood, a strange sound overpowers the loud horns and buses on Bethlehem Road.

"What's that, Daddy?" Amy asks.

"It's your stomach," Joel says, inviting a dirty look from his father. They stand up and look out the glass doors of the living room.

"That, my sweethearts, is the Pesach sacrifice," says Dick. "Mr. Abutbul has brought home the baby without blemish. We can watch it run around his roof and listen to it mehh for the next four days."

"I don't want to go to any sacrifice," Joel says, turning away from the window. He twirls his Red Sox cap as if it were a roulette wheel.

"Don't give me any lip, son. You're going and that's final."

"What's a blemish?" Amy asks.

"It's a scar or a cut, sweetheart, or a blind lamb or one with five legs. God only wants perfect specimens for his sacrifices . . . like you."

"What's a sacrifice, Daddy?" Amy asks. She molds her body into her father's chest and Dick holds her there lovingly.

"That's when you kill an animal and give it to God. Then God forgives your sins and loves you again. Or when you give up something you love very much to show God you love him more."

"Do you love God, Daddy?"

Dick looks at his four-year-old creation. He remembers the miracle of her birth, her first two months, when it wasn't clear she would make it. He loves the feel of her feathery hair under his palms.

"I love you, sweetheart."

"A sacrifice is when a guy bunts and there's another guy on base," Joel says and covers his laughter with his baseball cap.

Dick cuffs him on the head with a full hand.

Joel whines.

Amy puts her thumb in her mouth and twirls her hair.

Five minutes later the lamb is tied to the chimney on the roof opposite the Coens' living room, mehhing its head off.

"We're going to listen to this for four days?" Bonnie calls from the kitchen.

On Friday morning Bonnie is frantic because Rabbi Benstock has asked her to host three more students from Pardes for the Seder. "I wish you wouldn't go over there, Dick. I need your help." She is cleaning the Seder plate, the one given to them by their friends from B'nai Avraham. "Besides, I've never invited the Abutbuls over here."

"So what?" Dick says.

"So, we have so much work to do for the Seder."

"Don't worry, honey, we'll have time."

"It's inhumane."

"The way people drive here is inhumane." Dick kisses the back of her neck.

"Don't bite me," she says, rubbing her neck. "You can invite the Abutbuls for cake and coffee after the sacrifice."

Dick looks at the Seder plate in Bonnie's hands. He thinks of his friends back home, the Seders they held together each year. Once they even rented the grill room at the country club, so all the men could go straight to the Seder from the eighteenth hole. He wonders where his friends will be celebrating this year.

"Shouldn't you at least take them something? A bottle of wine?"

"I'm taking the kids."

Downstairs on Bethlehem Road at eleven in the morning, everyone in Baka is doing last-minute shopping before the Seder. This is Igor the butcher's high season. The shop is packed. Next door at Shmulik's laundry, people are waiting in line for their dry-cleaned pants and dresses for Pesach. Shmulik is the master of crumbs. He guarantees that if a customer finds one bread crumb or cookie crumb in a pocket, he will refund all payment. How many cleaners do that in Newton? On both sides of Bethlehem Road, cars are parked with one front wheel and one back wheel on the sidewalk, the other two wheels in the street. Everyone is blocking everyone else. Drivers scream, "Watch out!" "Go to hell!" "Maniac!" The entrance to Ben-Eli's corner grocery on the ground floor of Abutbul's building is blocked by cars.

In the field between Ben-Eli's grocery and Tikvatenu Synagogue on Zerubavel Alley, there is an area for grazing. Shepherds from Zur Bachar bring their small and straggly herds of sheep and goats. In the field this morning, fathers with their sons and daughters are bending over small fires. This must be the *chametz* shtick. Dick has never seen anything like it. Rabbi Diskin, the junior rabbi at Temple B'nai Avraham, called this part of the holiday "outdated" and "inappropriate for twentieth-century Newton," but here, across the street from Dick's own apartment, at least seven fathers are burning breadcrumbs and pieces of noodles that were swept up with feathers in candlelight.

The guys back home wouldn't believe this. Dick doesn't believe it himself. For a few months he had shared Bonnie's desire to be a player on the stage of Jewish history and therefore move to Israel. Now that he's lived here almost a year, he feels like he has fallen off the stage altogether and landed on a foreign set from a distant past, where everything, not only the language, is backward. There is no role for him to play in the world of animal sacrifice and burning breadcrumbs, other than witness. He grabs Joel's hand and Amy's arm before they cross the street.

"You kids ever see a Pesach like this in Boston?"

"You're hurting me, Daddy," says Amy. She lowers her foot into the street.

Dick pulls her back. "Do you want to get killed?"

"You're squeezing my hand, Dad," Joel says. "I hate Pesach."

"Hold on, son. Drivers here are crazy."

Dick leads his children across the street, stopping in the

middle for the number 6 bus to skim by. He pulls his children toward him. When they reach the opposite sidewalk, Amy turns around to look up at their apartment. Bonnie is at the window, waving.

"Look, Daddy. There's Mommy."

Dick and Joel turn and look up. They wave and smile. Dick acknowledges Bonnie's grimace with a fake smile.

He leads his kids to Abutbul's building, the first entrance on Rehov Reuven.

"Carry me, Daddy," Amy whines. "I'm tired."

"You're a big girl, Amy. What grade are you in now?" He feels embarrassed that he doesn't know exactly where his daughter is in the educational bureaucracy, but it is all so foreign to him, this Israeli system: kindergarten, pre-K, pre-pre-K. To think that you have to decide if a child is secular or religious at the age of four. If he had known more about the education his kids wouldn't get, maybe he would have encouraged Bonnie to wait with the aliyah thing until the kids were finished with high school. They could have learned about Pesach in Boston, like thousands of other Jews, and moved to Israel to die.

Dick vows to spend more time with Amy during Pesach vacation. Is it really three weeks? He will take her to the Medrano Circus that has pitched its tent over on Hebron Road, and to the Biblical Zoo.

"Pre-K, Daddy."

"And I'm going to the army next week, Pop."

Dick gives Joel's baseball cap a knock with his hand. Joel ducks this time.

"My hero," Dick says, trying to put a loving spin on it. He still wants to be a good father, especially to his son, his firstborn.

When Joel was born, Dick felt more empowered than when he had earned his degree as a chiropractor. He couldn't explain it. Being a father gave him a sense of mission, purpose, like nothing else. In the beginning, all he cared about was that his son should grow up to be a mensch. It was hard to set limits for the boy while at the same time showing how much he cared for him. In Israel, it was proving impossible. What's left is a goulash of limits Dick tries to set, flavored with Bonnie's overprotectiveness—*Don't touch the child.* Since they arrived in Israel, Dick has felt distanced from his son, who speaks Hebrew fluently and understands soccer. Dick can barely understand his patients when he asks them what hurts.

Inside the stairwell leading up to Abutbul's apartment, Dick tells Amy to hold on to the railing, to walk slowly, and not to let go until she reaches the top floor. High-pitched, piercing noises waft down from the open door to the roof.

"What's that?" Amy asks.

"It's your farts," Joel says and pushes her in the back.

"Cut the lip, buster," Dick says.

The hallway is dark. After three floors, they reach the roof, where the sudden light blinds them. The mehhing is so loud Amy covers her ears. Joel puts on sunglasses that his mother told him to take at the last minute.

The lamb is on its back on a dirty white canvas mat spread over most of the floor. Its two hind legs are tied with one rope and the front two legs with another. Amy twists her head to look at the lamb's upside-down face.

"He's so itsy-bitsy," she says. "Can I call him Itsy, Daddy?"

"Call him whatever you want, sweetheart." Dick approaches Abutbul.

"Why is he tied up, Dad?" Joel asks.

Mr. Abutbul, wearing jeans and a magenta T-shirt that says *ROMA* in black capital letters, greets Dick and shakes hands. Abutbul's feel like sandpaper. "Glad you made it, Dr. Coen."

"Call me Dick."

"For you this must be something. You don't do this in America, do you?"

"No, but we're all Jews."

"Right. Same father."

Dick doesn't know if Abutbul is referring to Abraham, Moses, or God, but he doesn't ask. Abutbul leans over and brushes his hand over Joel's baseball cap. Then he gives a little tug on Amy's ponytail.

"This is Joel," Dick says, "and Amy. Kids, this is Mr. Abutbul, our neighbor."

"Welcome," Abutbul says. "We celebrate Pesach. Like our forefathers in Egypt."

Amy and Joel look at their father. Dick winks at them.

Abutbul points to the man standing next to the lamb.

"Dr. Coen, meet Biton, the *shochet*. Biton," he shouts over the mehhing of the lamb, "my American neighbor, Dr. Coen."

Biton extends a hand and Dick shakes it. He has never met a ritual slaughterer before. The *shochet's* appearance repulses Dick. A stained white apron barely covers the man's enormous belly. His shirttails hang out one side of his pants, along with his ritual fringes. His pant cuffs are tucked into black rubber boots, making him look like a balloon. Stubble on his face reminds Dick of ashes, and his kippa, a black satin number, tilts onto his forehead, which is full of sweat.

Dick looks toward his apartment and sees Bonnie behind the closed kitchen window, watching.

"Wave to your mom, kids," he says. They run to the low wall encircling the roof and wave.

Biton nods to the children. "Only two?" he says to Dick.

"Only two."

The children return and cling to their father.

"Why's it peeing, Daddy?" Amy hides her face in her father's thigh.

"He has to go to the bathroom, just like you."

"Why is he tied up, Dad?" Joel repeats. He glances at his mother in the window. She is waving and moving her lips. "What is she saying, Dad?"

Dick is busy watching the *shochet* check the lamb for blemishes.

"Looks good to me," Biton tells Abutbul, then turns to the visitors. "Strange God we have. He wants animals without blemishes. Us, He forgives all our—How you say it?—comingshorts."

Dick has never thought of it that way and feels grateful that the *shochet* isn't just a butcher, that he is a thinking person. Though Dick himself cannot believe, he sometimes admires those who do.

"Is this a kid, Daddy?" Amy asks. "We learned the song 'Had Gad Yah ha ha ha, Had Gad Yah' in pre-K."

"A kid is a young goat," Joel declaims. "This is a lamb, a young sheep."

Dick notes his son's I'm-smarter-than-you tone. "My *chacham*," he says, looking at Abutbul and Biton.

"Is it a boy lamb or a girl lamb, Daddy?" Amy asks.

"Only boys for Pesach," says Abutbul. Dick marvels at his ability to express everything he needs to without complete sentences. He associates this ability with the scar on his chin but can't make any logical connection.

Biton walks over to a small wooden table next to the mehhing animal that is now struggling on its back to get free. On the table are a knife sharpener, scissors, a kitchen knife, a folded white towel package, and a saw.

"Why does the floor need a tablecloth, Daddy?" asks Amy.

"Clean tiles for Mrs. Abutbul," their host says and chuckles.

Amy runs back to the low wall encircling the roof. In terracotta-colored plastic containers on the floor along the wall are fragrant plants with soft green leaves and delicate white flowers.

"They're like snowflakes," Amy says, pointing to the flowers. She rubs the leaves like she has seen her mother do at the neighborhood nursery down the street.

"Hyssop," replies Abutbul.

Joel walks over to stand next to his sister. He leans over the low wall and sees all the cars parked on the sidewalk below on Bethlehem Road. Amy starts to inch her way up the wall. Joel grabs her arm and pulls her down. She cries.

"Don't touch her," Dick shouts. He goes to stand between them and holds their upper arms like chicken necks. "Wave to your mother," he commands. He waves their arms, as if his children are marionettes. The children don't smile. Dick nods to Bonnie, whose expression has turned somber. He turns to his kids and tells them he wants them to stand still, over there, far from the low wall, and just watch. This is a rare opportunity, he says. They are lucky. Not every child in Israel has seen the Pesach sacrifice just like it was done in Egypt thousands of years ago. Now they should settle down and be grateful, keep quiet, save their questions for later, and just watch.

The three of them walk to the edge of the white canvas floor mat, while Biton the *shochet* picks up the scissors from the wooden table. Biton walks toward the lamb. He grabs its head and holds it between his legs. With the scissors, Biton cuts the hair on the lamb's throat. The lamb tries to resist but can't. Amy tries to hide behind her father, but he pulls her out from behind his legs.

Abutbul turns on a faucet connected to a hose and takes the hose over to the lamb. He washes down the neck where Biton has cut the hair. The skin is soft and pink. Biton lets go of the sheep's head and the animal mehhs even louder now. Joel plays with his sunglasses. He tries to look out over the top rim. Dick tells him to stand still and stop fidgeting, to act like the nine-year-old he is, not a baby.

Biton lifts the clean white folded-towel package from the table as if it were an eight-day-old baby. He unfolds the towel. Inside is a black leather case. He opens the case. Inside is a knife with a black handle and a silver blade the size of a twelve-inch ruler. Joel straightens his glasses so he won't get blinded by the sheen of the blade.

"Look at that, kids. Will you just look at that," says Dick. "Isn't that the biggest knife you've ever seen?"

Joel twists the visor of his baseball cap and glances at his mother in the window across the street. She is waving.

Biton the *shochet* runs both edges of the knife against a fingernail on his left hand.

"Why's he doing that, Dad?" Joel whispers to his father.

"I don't know, son. Keep still and watch."

Biton walks over to the lamb's head. He holds the lamb's head back with his left hand and says some Hebrew words. Dick tries to decipher the words, but Biton speaks so fast, and with such an unfamiliar accent, that he can't make out what is being said. Then, like a magician, before Dick sees what is happening, Biton has drawn the knife across the soft pink skin. Blood bursts out like

EVERY MAN A LAMB

Joel's nosebleeds when he was five. It gushes onto the white canvas mat. Amy cries and hides her face in her father's leg. Joel squeezes his eyes shut.

My Israeli heroes, Dick thinks. He puts more pressure on Joel's arm. "Open your eyes, kid. Be a man."

Biton has let go of the lamb. It collapses on its side with a thump. Pools of deep magenta blood form around the lamb's neck. Its eyes are still open. Dick sees a certain sweetness in them, as if nothing has happened. *Itsy*, he thinks. Now the lamb begins to convulse, little shivers, as if it's trying to ward off flies. Amy peeks and when she sees this shaking, her crying increases. The lamb's whole head is covered with blood. Where there are large clots of blood, the color is richer, deeper. Dick can't take his eyes off the flow of the blood. The stains become puddles and the puddles rivulets. Dick releases his children so he can get closer to the lamb. Some of its blood spurts onto his hands.

Biton puts down the silver knife on the table and picks up the kitchen knife. He begins to skin the lamb, starting with the testicles. Blood covers his hands and his apron. His black boots are drenched in blood.

In between her sobs, Amy begs to go home.

"Yeah, Dad, let's go," Joel adds. "I'm going to vomit."

"This is your heritage, kids. I want you to know where you come from."

Joel starts walking toward the door of the roof.

"Where are you going, young man?" Dick calls after him. "Get back here. We're not done yet." He feels like he has entered another realm of being, that the Dick Coen here on the roof is different from the Dick Coen who lives across the street. He doesn't understand what's happening to him. He just knows he has to be here with his kids, as if he was destined to be here with them, as if it's in his genetic makeup. Maybe this is why he made aliyah.

Amy runs to the low wall and inches her way up. "Mommy, Mommy," she yells, "they killed the lamb."

Bonnie, from behind the closed window, motions her daughter to get down.

Dick runs toward Amy and grabs her from her waist. "Get down, you little . . ." he yells.

"Don't hurt the child," Abutbul calls to him.

He pulls down his daughter with both hands and gets blood on her dress. She falls and starts to cry.

"Leave her alone, Dad," Joel butts in. He runs from the door to his sister. "Don't touch her."

Dick pushes him away, getting blood on Joel's shirt as well.

"My heroes, my big Israeli heroes," Dick says.

Biton and Abutbul are busy skinning the lamb and checking to see if all its organs are intact. Biton lifts up the lining, holds the lamb's balls away from its body. Then he cuts them off.

"Let's get out of here," Joel yells.

"Be a man," Dick shouts.

Joel pushes his sister and runs to the puddles of blood on the canvas. He bends down and plunges both his hands into the blood. He rubs the blood into his hands, shouting, "Like this, Dad? Like this? Is this what you want? An Israeli man?" Then he gets up and goes over to the low wall. He shakes the blood from his hands over the ledge onto the people and the cars on the sidewalk below. They look up and laugh, thinking it is water from a hose. Then they yell. Amy throws her arms around Joel's waist and pulls him away from the wall. "Don't hurt anyone," Amy wails. "Stop it." She runs to the door and cries, "I want to go home, Daddy. I want to go home."

Biton and Abutbul, busy skinning the lamb, give Dick a look: *Can't control the kids?* Dick slaps his son's face with his bloodied hand. He glances across the street at Bonnie. Now she is sitting at the window with both hands covering her mouth.

"I want to go home, Daddy," Amy moans.

"We'll go when it's over."

Biton has removed the small penis and slit open the belly. He is pushing his arm inside the cavity of the lamb to touch its lungs. "Only if its lungs are intact is it a kosher animal," he says, looking at Dick.

After Biton confirms that it is kosher, he tells Abutbul that he and his family and their guests have to roast the meat and eat it by midnight to fulfill the biblical injunction. Abutbul walks to the planter. Joel runs to the closed door to stand next to Amy. Abutbul picks three sprigs of hyssop and walks back to the bloody carcass. He dips the hyssop into the pool of blood on the white canvas. Then he walks over to the door and paints the lintel and the doorposts with the blood of the lamb. Some of the blood drips onto Amy's ponytail and Joel's shirt.

"Daddy, Daddy," Amy calls.

"Dad," says Joel, "let's go home."

"No Egypt?" Abutbul looks at his new neighbor. Then he tells the children that the Israelites painted their doorposts with blood so the Angel of Death, who came to slaughter the first-born Egyptians, would pass over the homes of the Israelites. "The first Pesach," he concludes, ecstatic.

"This hard for Americans, Dr. Coen," Abutbul says, and Dick isn't sure if it's a question or a statement. "My kids helped. Now they big. No patience now."

Dick is beginning to wonder how he will explain this to Bonnie, how she will react when she sees the blood on their clothes and in their hair, why he became violent with them. He loves his children. He doesn't want to hurt them. He doesn't know what happened.

Dick heads for the hose to wash off his hands. "Come here," he calls to the kids. "I'll wash your hands of all this blood." His voice is softer now, calmer. "Put your hands here under the hose." They obey. "We'll go home now, I promise." His children's hands are soft and pink.

As water washes away the blood, he thinks of B'nai Avraham and the country club and the lamb, especially its eyes. Something is different. Dick feels something new. For the time being, he names it contrition.

"Come here," he calls again to the kids, even though they are standing next to him. "We must wash our hands of all this blood."

He apologizes to Abutbul for their behavior.

"No problem. A happy and kosher Pesach," Abutbul says.

"To all the children of Abraham," Dick adds. "Thank you, and thank you, Biton."

The *shochet* doesn't look up. He is in a frenzy of skinning and cutting and checking, sweat dripping from his forehead into his eyes and onto the carcass of the lamb.

Dick stretches out his arm, pushes open the door, and leads his children out. He holds their hands in the dark stairwell, trying to be gentle as they walk down. Only Amy's muffled sobs pierce the silence. Clutching their small hands, Dick feels a love for his children stronger and more tender than ever before.

When they are downstairs on the sidewalk, Dick rubs his eyes. The air smells of smoke from the small fires across the street. He asks his children if they want a falafel from Ovadia's. "The last *chametz* before Pesach. Let's go for it."

Amy and Joel stand together, looking in silence at the fires across the street.

"Half pita or whole," Dick persists. He wants to give his children something good, a special treat.

"No," says Joel, as if the Red Sox lost a home game and will always lose their home games.

"Me neither," says Amy, putting her thumb in her mouth.

"Don't move," Dick says. "I'll go get us a whole pita. We'll share." He runs over to Ovadia's, but it's already closed for Pesach. When he returns to Joel and Amy, they are standing exactly where he left them. He is taken aback by their submission.

"Come on," he says, feigning enthusiasm. "Let's show these drivers who's boss." He tells his children to latch onto his belt so they can cross the street together. "It's a jungle out here," he says. Amy reaches up and grabs his left side. Joel holds on to his right.

The three stand at the curb on the corner of Bethlehem Road and Reuven. Dick tells them to look to the left and then to the right. Their three heads move in unison.

Then Joel looks up toward their apartment across the street. "Where's Mom?" he murmurs.

Dick looks up. Bonnie is gone, the window a pane of clean glass reflecting the noon sun. He feels a sudden weakness in his legs, as if his spine might surrender to Bethlehem Road. He shudders when a loud horn uproots him from his sinking feeling. With his children linked as one body, Dick steps slowly into the street, praying, for what feels like the first time, that nobody gets hurt.

Igor the Butcher

My wife is always telling me my hands smell like
chickens. She won't come near me 'cause I stink.
Soon I'll retire and buy new hands. I'll sell the
shop and move to Bat Yam. It's nice there, near the
sea. My son has a shop there. He sells buttons. He
didn't want any part of the butcher shop, not the
neck, the feet, not even the gizzard.

This one guy upstairs, he orders through me a
lamb every year before Pesach. What am I going to
tell him? That Jews don't do such things anymore?
That the Temple was destroyed two thousand years
ago? That the roof is common property and nobody
wants lamb blood seeping into their apartment?

There's no house committee, and even if there
was, nobody would agree to anything. Nobody here
wants his neighbor to have more of anything than he
has. You understand me? Love thy neighbor? Hah.
Here it's more like Block your neighbor, Don't pay
house dues, Steal his garden. So what can I do? I
order him the lamb.

You know the Ingathering of the Exiles? What a
mistake that was!

GET OUT OF JAIL

Just before the fallopian curve, Pat collapses on the chipped stair. She transfers her turquoise purse from her back to her chest.

"Come home, Ema," her daughter calls from the porch balcony twelve steps above. The little girl is climbing the balustrade.

Pat looks down. On Bethlehem Road a bus driver is honking at a silver car trying to turn into Rehov Shimshon, where a cement mixer is blocking traffic. Baka has become a Monopoly board on which buyers build on biblical streets—Shimshon, Gid'on, Boaz, and Yael. All this in the shadows of the Electric Company and Railroad. Pat just paid her Hospital Tax. Now it's time to Go to Jail.

"Come home, Ema," her daughter whines, climbing down the balustrade and racing down the stairs. She tugs at the outside pocket on her mother's purse. Pat tells her to let go, teetering on the stair. She pushes her daughter's hand off her purse. She is exhausted from the long drive, the heat, the world. The three-year-old leads her up the twelve remaining stairs. If the doctor's typist had finished Pat's release letter at ten instead of two, the homecoming would have looked different. Hezi would have brought her home instead of a cab driver who took the turns too fast. She'd be relaxed. Maybe.

"Did you bring me a surprise from the hotel?" her daughter asks.

Pat hasn't seen her for three weeks.

"Hospital, not hotel," says Pat.

The child's small hand clutches the hem of Pat's skirt.

"Where's your brother?" Pat asks as she unloads her overnight case and new purse in the entrance hall. She feels a painful familiarity when she sees the cheap reproduction of Winslow Homer's *The Wrecked Schooner*. The forlorn vessel reminds her of the two-hour class she took with her mother at the St. Louis Museum.

The little girl runs into the children's bedroom and tells her brother to stop playing. "Ema is home," she says, "Ema is home." The boy continues practicing "Hatikvah" on his recorder. "Ema's home!" she screams.

He takes the recorder out of his mouth and walks to the entrance hall barefoot, the wet instrument in his left hand.

"Hey, dear. I'm home," says Pat, forcing a smile. She approaches the boy to give him a kiss on the cheek, but he turns away, and as he turns some of the saliva from the recorder shpritzes onto her cheek.

"Great," he says, "I'm practicing," and he goes back to the national anthem in his room. Facing his bed, he shouts to remind her that she owes Shira four hundred lira for last month's lessons and that the Independence Day program is in ten days.

Pat tries a long breath, but her insides still hurt. She walks deeper into the apartment, surveying the mess in the living room— crusts of bread, peeled crayons, empty Bugs Bunny plates with dried bits of grape jam and chewed pieces of corn schnitzel. On the kitchen counter, a bread knife, plastic dinosaur, and Mickey Mouse cup next to a puddle of milk. She goes straight to her bedroom without passing Go, without collecting two hundred lira.

On the door is a sign in black letters: BARUCH HA'BA, EMA.

Instead of an exclamation point, there is a flower with a hot-pink stem and three yellow petals shaped like wombs. No pistil.

"I drew that," pipes the three-year-old, who is clinging to her knee like a third leg.

The sign is taped to the aliyah poster, a photomontage of an ancient olive oil lamp sprouting a modern test tube. *Our Future Is Where Our Past Is.* Pat recognizes the hand of Mazal, the downstairs neighbor, who works as a cleaning lady in the Ministry of Absorption. Mazal deposits all things aliyah and in English at Pat's apartment.

"Nice flower," Pat says to her little girl. "Who did the Hebrew?"

If she were a good mother, she would kiss her three-year-old's head for the flower and teach her first grader the difference between feminine and masculine gender in Hebrew. But she is tired, extremely tired, and wants only to sleep.

In her bedroom she puts her purse on her bed. Squished in the inside pocket in a white plastic hospital bag is her uterus. The cervix, with its cauliflower motif, was sent to pathology, along with a carpaccio of the uterine wall. From her hospital bed on the seventh floor, she saw thousands of wild cats pounce and scramble into the vast green garbage bin, vying for the best meat. Her organ would not be part of that game.

If she were the High Priest in the Temple, she would offer her womb as a sacrifice to the Lord of Hosts. And if she were independently wealthy, she would buy the forlorn Allenby Camp on Hebron Road, tear it down, get a mortgage, and build two houses, one for herself and one next door for her husband and kids. But she is only Pat, victim of cervical cancer, object of a radical hysterectomy called the Wertheim procedure.

Her mother had wanted to name her Pearl, after her own mother, but such an old-fashioned name did not resonate in suburbia, so mother and father compromised on Patsy. By third grade, she had lost the "sy." "Pat" worked, until she played around with Israel's Sephardi men and married one.

Pat lies down on the bed and her daughter joins her.

She closes her eyes and thinks of her name, how Hezi had a problem with it, how he said "Pat? *Shmech Pat?*" the first time they met at a folk dancing club, how it came out as *Pot* with his Afulan accent, how Mazal called her *Poht*, which meant "cunt" in Hebrew, how her son's principal called her *Paht*, which meant "breadcrumb." She felt crummy. Now, without a uterus, she would go to the Ministry of Interior and change her name to Winslow, but first she must sleep.

After their first anniversary, Hezi shortened the family name from Rachamim ("compassion") to Rachmi ("my uterus"). It took two years of marriage for her to realize that her promiscuity had been an expression of a deeper need, a need unfulfilled in the marriage. She called it love, but when she raised the issue with Hezi, he accused her of being "too American."

Hezi enters the apartment by slamming the front door. He sees no dinner on the dining room table and goes into a rage. "I take care of kids for three fucking weeks. Dinner on table every night at six thirty. Where is the *kavod*?" He yells all this in his unique blend of Hebrew and English in the living room while the television blares the Arabic news. Nobody's watching. The son is still practicing "Hatikvah" behind his closed door and Pat is lying on the bed with her shoes on, her daughter next to her, humming a song about King George Street. The purse lies between them.

Hezi's shrieks penetrate Pat like cries of hungry crows. If she were a good wife, there would be Moroccan fish simmering on the stove, or warm greasy Yemenite *malawah* waiting in the oven, the table set for four, Hezi at the head.

He bursts into the bedroom, throwing his briefcase onto the floor. "Haven't you rested enough? Doctor Uptownsky . . ."

"Uptonsky," Pat murmurs.

"Uptonsky. Downtonsky. I don't give a shit. He said in no time you'd be back to normal."

She turns her head to her husband, who has indeed kept the family intact these three weeks. She apologizes for staying so long at the Plaza Hotel, but the service was so fine, sheets of pure silk, gourmet soups, she felt so divinely spoiled. She apologizes for the E. coli infection that invaded her system on day eight, when she was due to be released. She apologizes for the inconvenient railroad track slashed into her belly from navel to pubis.

Pat knows that Hezi's anger has to get out of his system, if not today then tomorrow, and if not tomorrow then the day after. She knows, too, that after this burst will come tenderness, just as chapter two follows one. He will call her *ahuvati*, as if playing the loving husband in a black-and-white movie, and he will touch her dirty-blonde hair with gentleness, even awe. It's just a matter of time. She knows her man.

If she owned Park Place, she would call the maid to come

clean and cook meals for the next ten days. But she is the bad wife of the man with the bad mother who sent little Hezi to a kibbutz when he was five years old, and then let him come home when he was eight to sleep in her bed.

Pat sits up on her bedspread and arranges her new turquoise purse on her chest. From behind, the little girl jumps up and throws her arms around Pat's neck.

"Piggy back, piggy back," she cries.

"Careful," says Pat. "I'm fragile."

That night, when Pat rolls down the bedspread and crawls into bed, she notices the same floral sheets as when she left for the hospital. No problem. A man can only do so much. At least he didn't forget the little girl at nursery school or in the car. At least he fed the son each afternoon before he left the house to play with friends. And hadn't Hezi taken them to Afula for Passover, while she ate hard-boiled eggs at Hadassah Hospital? So what if her mother-in-law never visited her.

Pat puts her face into her 100 percent duck-down pillow. In the hospital she missed this one luxury item, given to her by her mother three years earlier, when she came for the little girl's birth. Well, not exactly the birth. Her mother had hung around Jerusalem waiting for Pat to deliver. When the due date slipped by with no sign, her mother hopped over to Istanbul to shop. She loved Turkish rugs. She would have been in Jerusalem for the hysterectomy, but she had signed up for a Jewish Roots Tour. "You know, sweetheart," she had explained, "Warsaw, Auschwitz, that stuff . . . But I'll be thinking of you." Now, as the pillow embraces her face like soft hands, images from last month fill her with sadness: the pink discharge, the doctor's dinnertime call with results of the Pap smear, her mother sending a purse.

She turns her head to Hezi's side and the dream comes back, the post-op dream, when the zonda tube was still stuffed down her esophagus for "airway management," as Uptonsky explained.

There was a large, dark, empty two-story house. Bare walls, no furniture, no people. She floats upstairs and finds a garret under a thatch roof. In the garret is a chair and a single bed with a straw mattress, the kind used by nuns sworn to silence. She sits on the straight-backed chair and looks out the closed triangular window. A raging river rushes by. Its speed and force scare her. If she opens the window, she will drown.

Whose house is this?

She had wanted to cry but couldn't because her stitches hurt and the intubation blocked her airways. "Your husband slept on the floor over there in the corner all night," the social worker said in the morning, pointing to the empty corner. "He cares. Not all husbands do that."

Pat had felt weak, confused, maybe still drugged from the anesthetics. *Whose house is empty?*

Now, in her own bedroom, on her beloved pillow, she struggles to find a comfortable position for her vanquished body. She is a country that has been ravaged, but everyone's calling it victory. She closes her eyes and sees an enormous mouth with two fallopian tubes adjacent to the exterior wall. The upstairs windows are empty eyes.

At midnight she awakens to the hum of the TV from the living room. Hezi has probably fallen asleep on the couch in front of a rerun of the seven-week epic *Pillar of Fire: The Incredible Story of Israel's Rebirth*. She fingers her incision. The stitches stick out like a feathered zipper. She feels nothing. Feeling will return in a few weeks, Uptonsky promised. Nerves have to heal. "*Hakol yavo l'mkomo b'shalom*," he said, quoting the Talmud. Everything will fall into place.

Wasn't there a less intrusive way to reach the uterus and cervix? Why didn't she question and research before going under the knife? How long will she be passive? She turns onto her other side slowly, gently, insecure in her new house. She closes her eyes, relieved that her precious purse sits on the floor next to her with its treasure inside.

At three thirty, something pushes and pulls her arm.

"Ema, can I go potty?"

Since when does the little girl need permission to pee?

"Yes," Pat murmurs from half sleep, "then back to bed." She maneuvers her body toward Hezi, who is snoring.

Minutes later the child is back pulling her arm again. "Ema, wipe me."

"You're big, sweetheart," she says, turning her body again like a foreign object, this time toward her daughter. "Wipe yourself."

"The paper fell on the floor," the little girl whispers loudly. A hiss of warm air comes from her mouth onto Pat's face. Where is the call button for a nurse?

"My slippers," Pat says, putting her body in a sitting position.

The child slides them with her bare feet to the side of the bed. Pat slips them on and shuffles into the bathroom, eyes half closed, holding the little girl's hand.

In the bathroom, lit by a Minnie Mouse nightlight, Pat sees her turquoise purse on the floor in front of the potty. Both pockets are ripped open. Her wallet is unzipped and several coins are strewn on the floor in front of the washing machine. Next to the bathtub is the white plastic bag from the hospital. Along the top edge, baby teeth have made cuts, releasing a putrid smell.

"Wipe me," says the little girl, returning to the potty, her pajama bottoms falling to her feet.

"What have you done?" Pat cries, eyes opening wide. "What did you do?"

"Made in potty," the child says.

"Who told you to take my purse? You took my purse. Look what you've done."

Pat shuts the door to the bathroom.

"Didn't want to potty by myself," says the little girl. "What's that?" She points to the plastic bag full of her teeth marks. "Is a BM inside?"

"You have no business taking my purse, young lady. Grandma sent that to me." Pat balances herself with one hand on the sink and tries bending at the knees to pick up the punctured bag. "This is Ema's special purse from Grandma. You're a bad girl." She feels herself coiling out of control. She wants her three-year-old to feel guilty.

"What's inside," the little girl says, looking between her legs into the potty.

"Nothing's inside." Pat turns the purse inside out and shakes it in front of her face. "It's empty," she shouts. "Can't you see? It's empty."

The little girl sits frozen on the potty, her pajamas circling her feet like a puddle. Pat lowers herself to sit on the rim of the bathtub. She clutches the empty thing to her chest. From low in her empty gut behind the stitches a cry begins, but it still hurts too much to cry. She covers the pain with her hands. The little girl doesn't move.

"I could wring your neck," Pat says. Her voice is soft, but the words scare them both. Pat doesn't know where they are coming from, to whom they belong. "Come here, get up," she commands. The little girl doesn't move. "I said, come here, get up." The little girl with her pajamas around her feet stands up and almost falls onto her mother. Pat grips her bare shoulders with her hands and starts shaking her. "If I tell you not to do something, then don't do it. Do you hear me?"

She shakes the little girl, whose head shakes as if it might fall off her flimsy neck.

The child begins to cry, "I'm sorry, I'm sorry, Ema."

"Be quiet. You'll wake up your father." The little girl cries louder; Pat tightens her grip and shakes harder. "Shut up, I said."

"What's going on?" Hezi's voice comes from the other side of the door, as if he is still asleep. He pushes the bathroom door ajar and stands in the hallway. When he sees his half-naked daughter, he steps into the bathroom and grabs a bath towel from the rod over Pat's head. The rod falls out of its hinges and hits Pat and the little girl on their heads.

"Shit!" Pat yells, standing up and rubbing her head. "Nothing works in this cursed house." She grabs her daughter's shoulders again and shakes her. "Everything's gone, gone."

Hezi touches her arm and she releases the child from her grip. The little girl flops down onto the potty.

Hezi puts a hand on Pat's shoulder. "Calm down, sweetheart," he says. "What happened?"

"She emptied my purse, the one my mother sent me." Pat sits back down on the rim of the bathtub, her hands covering her incision.

"Come, Pat." Hezi's voice is full of compassion. "You're tired."

He lifts her up from under her arms. "It's been a long day. A hard three weeks." She sinks into his body.

"Hold me."

He holds her while her body heaves. Mixed with her tears are words coming from the empty dark place within.

"I want . . . my . . . mommy." Her voice trembles.

The little girl gets up from the potty and clutches her father's leg.

Pat feels the presence of her son standing behind the half-open door to the bathroom, listening.

"I'm sorry," she whispers to Hezi.

"Come, let's go back to bed." He sits his wife down on the rim of the bathtub, wipes the little girl, and pulls up her pajamas. "You get back into bed now, sweetie."

The little girl throws her arms around his neck. "Abba, take me to bed."

He carries her off to bed. Pat raises her body to leave the bathroom. She sees her son standing in the dark hallway. She looks at him but says nothing. His eyes pierce the purse dangling from her chest.

Ten days later, Pat leaves her house to walk to Geulim School for the Independence Day program. Going down the staircase is easy, but the five-block walk is the longest she's taken since she came home from the hospital. Not only are the sidewalks broken and chipped, but the municipality has opened up Bethlehem Road to lay new telephone wires. Every year around Independence Day her street becomes an open wound, a raw cut in the fabric of the everyday.

Drivers honk; pedestrians curse. Pat walks slowly, watching each step. At the corner vegetable store, Herzl is arranging the oranges. He sees Pat and asks how she's doing. "Not exactly winning the jackpot, but I'll be OK," she says. When she passes Boris the shoemaker, she notes his newly painted sign: TIKUN NA'ALAYIM. She wishes her soul were as easy to fix as a sole. Opposite Rehov Shimon she rests on a wooden bench where usually only old people sit. She takes the turquoise purse from her back and clutches it to her chest.

As she approaches the school from Ingathering of the Exiles Street, Pat sees the first graders at recess. The equipment in the school's playground is broken and the geraniums planted along the walls of the school have been uprooted. Her son is chasing a friend. When he notices her, he continues running after his friend. She could have stayed home, she wants to tell him. Dragging her body this distance is not easy. She's here for him. The least he could do is wave.

Pat walks into the gym. Five rows of benches are arranged in a semicircle. The first three rows are for grades one through three, the last two for parents. Between the front row and the wall of the gym is the makeshift stage. Pat nods to some of the mothers she recognizes from parent meetings and sits by herself on the back bench.

She watches Shira, the music teacher, arrange three stands for the children playing instruments. The principal, with the blinding orange hair and ivory cigarette holder, is instructing the gym teacher to call in the kids. The gym reeks of sweat. She regrets that her children do not have the facilities and opportunities she had in Clayton, Missouri, but when the rowdy children start filing in, dressed in blue jeans and white shirts, she remembers why she's here.

Her son, who ran freely only five minutes earlier, walks stiffly into the gym, holding his recorder like a sword, and sits down in the front row. When the third graders file in, pushing and screaming, the teacher sends one of the rambunctious boys to sit in the far corner of the gym by himself. Pat scans the other mothers, wondering if the boy's mother is present. Three fathers are in the audience, one wearing a uniform of the Knesset Guard, the other two smoking unlit cigarettes. When the children settle down to a low hum, the principal puts her own cigarette holder into her pocket and welcomes everyone to the program celebrating Israel's thirty-sixth Independence Day.

"This year we mark the celebration by saluting Gedera, the first Bilu settlement founded in 1884, exactly one hundred years ago."

Pat has heard of Bilu. She knows it's a Hebrew acronym that stands for something. The principal instructs the children to sit quietly without fidgeting or else they will find themselves on the floor in the corner. Even the parents are unruly. The principal hands over the program to Shira, the music teacher, who invites the second and third graders to the stage. She places them in a line facing the audience and hands them their costumes. The girls slip on long colorful skirts and tie scarves on their heads. The boys put on black belts and *kova tembles*, the iconic kibbutz hat. Then Shira takes out plastic farm tools from a carton and gives each child a tool. They are ready to begin.

These children are the student idealists who left Russia after the pogroms in the early 1880s and came to farm the Land of Israel. Shira explains that they are the founding mothers and fathers of Gedera, members of the Bilu organization, which means "House of Jacob, let us go up."

Go up they did, from the violence in Russia to the rocks in the Promised Land.

"Even on an empty stomach we did our work in the fields from morning to night," orate three second-grade girls holding rakes.

"The hard work did not ruin our spirit," say two boys with saws.

"We were happy, happy going into the fields and happy to return at night," say all the second- and third-grade children in unison.

Parents in the last two rows stretch their necks and ears. The microphone does not work. Shira motions to the gym teacher to flick a switch on the wall next to the door, but no luck. She asks the little pioneers to repeat their lines in a loud voice, which they do.

A boy steps forward carrying a shovel. "We had no running water, no electricity. All we had was courage and . . ." Shira mouths the word to him in a loud whisper from the wrinkled script she holds in her hand. "Oh yeah," says the boy, "all we had was courage and vision."

The audience laughs.

Pat wishes she had courage and vision like the Bilu pioneers of 1884. She thought she had them in 1974 when she first came to Israel, but over the years what she called vision unwound like an old bandage. Courage? The word doesn't exist in her vocabulary, neither in English nor in Hebrew.

If Grandma Pearl had joined the Bilu in Russia and settled in Gedera instead of St. Louis, Pat would have grown up Israeli. Maybe Pearl's great-grandson will mature into a man with courage and vision, will go out to the fields in the morning with happiness and return happy at night. But today, Pat has no idea how to imbue her son with this ideal. She feels like she has given him nothing and has nothing to give. A wrecked schooner, all around.

"We farmed grapes and wheat. Later we farmed oranges," say four girls, two holding plastic grapes and two plastic oranges.

"Gedera is known for its good air," say all the girls like a Greek chorus.

The parents smile and cough.

Now the children in costume, along with those on the benches, sing a song. "*Anu banu artza l'vnot u'lehibanot bah.*" We came to the land to build and to be rebuilt. The parents join in and start clapping. The children raise their right hands in fists for the final *bah*, as if to emphasize their will.

Pat remembers learning these words in the Hebrew *ulpan* during her first four months in Israel. What has she built, besides two children? Her accounting is meager. Been rebuilt? Became a mother. She has not fulfilled the Zionist dream of coming up into the motherland, building it and thereby being rebuilt. Only two kids? What else? She feels lonely and vulnerable.

The principal praises the children and says something about never forgetting the heritage of Gedera and the Bilu, about Geulim's vision of a playground that won't be vandalized. The grand finale is about to begin. Shira moves the three music stands toward the audience. Pat's son stands at the front, along with two other first graders. One is holding a triangle, one an accordion, and Pat's son a recorder. Shira opens the sheet music on the stands and turns to the audience.

"Please rise for 'Hatikvah.'"

Everyone rises. Pat stands up and holds her stomach. The incision is beginning to hurt, nerves coming back to life. She cannot see her son but hears his recorder. She sings the words softly to herself so she can concentrate on his playing. No mistakes. She shifts her body slightly to the left to get a glimpse of her boy. His white shirt needs ironing. Why didn't she take care of this yesterday? She had time. Why? Why? Guilt seizes her as she sings the national anthem. His performance is perfect.

Nefesh Yehudi homiyah, as long as a Jewish soul yearns. Pat thinks about her Jewish soul and how it never stops yearning for the next place, how she wishes it would settle down already since she has returned to the Homeland after two thousand years of exile, fulfilled the dream. Is she destined to yearn another two thousand? Can't she give it a rest?

While the audience sings, Pat realizes this Jewish longing covers a deeper, vaguer longing inside her. Is it for her mother? Hezi? Another child? She is not sure, but these questions make her tremble. She tries to hold herself together, not to cry in her son's gym, full of his friends, teachers, and principal. She does not want to embarrass him, yet feels that this moment may be her pinnacle, that all her previous decisions, which seemed random at the time, had a purpose, that the purpose was her standing here this morning in this pathetic gym, listening to her son play the national anthem with no mistakes on a puny recorder. This boy of hers, who barely talked, whom she barely knew, was the goal of her life and she had not known it. How blind she had been, tuned only to herself. No wonder she feels unloved. What is she doing? Where is *her* love? Why isn't she showing it every day of the week, every hour of the day, to her children, to Hezi?

When the song ends, she starts clapping. "Bravo! Bravo!" she yells in her American accent. "Hurrah, hurrah," she shouts in perfect English. She continues clapping until the principal raises her palms signaling enough.

But it will never be enough. It can never be enough. She waves to her son with both hands as if he might leave her. She gives him a thumbs-up. He does not respond. He and the other two children bow, close their music books, and join their classmates on the bench facing the gym wall.

If her mother had loved her the way she needed to be loved, she would have been standing next to her today, kvelling from Pearl's talented great-grandson who played the Israeli national anthem with no mistakes, for a crowd of yearning Jews.

But her mother is back in St. Louis playing mahjong and she is Pat Rachmi, a small crest in an enormous wave of immigrants, wife of Hezi, mother of two. She gathers herself to leave, thinking that with renewed vision and courage, she can still make her life work, she can renovate her family. She need not wait for anything or anyone. She will iron her son's shirt, cook healthy meals, talk to her daughter about her own irrational outburst. She will be patient and wait until they reply. She will go up to the motherland. She will sew and play board games, read her children books in whatever language they wish, and sing and dance. She will learn to hug them and never again raise a hand against them. She will call them by their names. She will go around the board, for however long it takes, until she gets out of jail.

After the performance, Pat walks up to her son and taps him on the shoulder. "You were great," she says, biting her lip, touching his blond curls, as if they were a fragile gift.

"Thanks, Ema," he says.

She notices his loose tooth on his lower jaw and she notices, too, that this is the first time she's heard him call her Ema since she came back from the hospital.

On the way home, Pat walks slowly, as if in a trance. She stops to inspect the small white blossoms on the trees along Bethlehem Road. They are on the verge of opening. How do they do it by themselves?

Farther down the road someone is finally cleaning the filthy windows of the post office. Pat crosses Rehov Yehuda and is happy to see that Moshe's newsstand is advertising a new photocopying machine. Only fifteen *agorot* a page. Across the street, Menachem has gone crazy. He's selling a dozen cheese *bourekas* for the price of eight.

The municipality has even distributed new plastic green dumpsters for each house. With luck, the Community Chest will announce the coming of the Messiah.

At the bench where she sat only an hour earlier, Pat takes off her purse and slips her ID card into her left chest pocket. Then she takes out the sealed plastic bag, "Property of Hadassah Hospital." She gives the universe a wink and, standing in front of the next green dumpster, Pat watches the trajectory of the plastic bag as it leaves her hand, sails into the spring air, and lands in the bin, an ideal curve, smooth as a mother's breast.

Boris, the Basement Shoemaker

You need a new tongue? No problem. I make shoes in the court of the Tsar. You know? In Russia. Once I make a pair of shoes for Rasputin. You know him? I never saw him personally, but his servant brought me the order and he said it was for Rasputin. He had a very large foot, you know? And a bunion on his left toe, so he needed special order. I used the finest leather in the shop, something I bought from my connection in Poland, but the Polack said the leather came from Italy. Who knows? A cow is a cow.

That was a beautiful pair of shoes. When my little boy saw them he wanted the same thing, shoes like Rasputin's. I promised him when things calmed down I'd make him a pair just like Rasputin's. Things never calmed down. There was the revolution. You know the Russian Revolution? That was a long time ago and thank God my son escaped the army and took a boat, a big boat for many people, to America. Now he's safe in Teaneck—that's New Jersey, this Teaneck—with all my grandchildren and he doesn't want any part of Jerusalem. No, he's never even come to visit. He says he's American now and the only shoes he wears are sneakers by Adid something or other. Those aren't real shoes.

HOMECOMING, 1982

I stood in the kitchen, neck crooked right, yelling at Les in Lebanon on the other end of the receiver. Ori writhed in the cradle of my left arm, his mouth attached to my left nipple. He sucked and paused with the rise and fall of my voice and I was pissed that son and father were pulling me in opposite directions.

"You're close to the border," I shouted, my inflection converting the statement to a question. "Sharon said we're only going in forty kilometers." The late-summer sun pounded on the window over the stove. Jerusalem, the city I loved, lounged in its Shabbat peace like lovers after sex.

"What border?" Les screamed back. Motors rumbled behind him and men shouted, "*Yallah, yallah*. We all have families on the home front." I imagined dust and sweat mingling with the smell of homesickness.

"The northern border," I shouted. Did Ori need a burp? Should I try to hook him back on the right side? The spit-up diaper wasn't near the phone. If I went for burping, he'd spit up all over me and the floor.

"So why am I looking down on Beirut?" Les yelled back, mad.

How the hell did I know why he was looking down on Beirut? My hands were full. Maybe Sharon lied. What did I know? This was only my second war, my first as wife and new mother. As I maneuvered Ori onto my shoulder, the receiver dropped. "Shoot."

"What are you shooting about?" My husband's voice rose from the floor and filled the kitchen. I imagined his voice flying through the August air, overlooking Beirut and then Jerusalem, as I squatted to pick up the receiver without dropping Ori.

"I dropped the phone," I said. "What time is it?"

"How the hell do I know, Kate? I haven't slept for seventy-two hours and they're sending me into Beirut tomorrow."

I hooked Ori onto the right side and he sucked peacefully. I asked Les why, what would he be doing there?

"I'm the guy who's collecting the wounded," he said, his voice softer now and edgy. "Driving an armored vehicle, picking up soldiers."

I heard "shoulders" and mentioned mine ached and asked when he'd be home. I sort of wanted him to come home already, after two months in Lebanon. But only sort of.

"A moving target," he said.

He sounded scared. Did he think he might die tomorrow in Beirut? Maybe he was calling to say goodbye. I had never heard him sound scared. He was always self-assured, excited to be defending the Jewish state, fulfilling his Zionist dream. Les, scared? "You'll make peace for Galilee," I said and felt dumb as soon as the stupid name of the war that wasn't even called a war, but an operation, left my mouth.

He asked how Ori was, his voice faraway, as if he were lost in the cedars above the city, ignoring the pushy loud soldiers vying for their turn on the phone.

"Fine." I didn't want to go into details, cry on his shoulder. It was enough taking care of everything by myself.

A loud boom sounded somewhere. Ori opened his eyes, let go of the nipple, looked at me for clues, and, when there were none, cried. I looked out the kitchen window to see if the explosion was nearby in Jerusalem. But, of course, it was Lebanon, near Les. "Was that a bomb?"

"No, sweetheart. It's Fourth of July at the Beirut Country Club ... Give the little bugger a kiss from his abba," he said and hung up, as I remembered to say good luck.

There was probably a Zionist protocol for this role of soldier's wife and new mother, but I didn't know it. Nobody taught it at *ulpan*. There were no "How to Cope" columns in the easy-Hebrew weekly. I knew I was supposed to put the needs of the soldier and the State of Israel above my own, but when my first baby was three months old, I couldn't. I was so absorbed in his every breath and burp that everyone else seemed secondary, even my soldier husband waiting on a Lebanese hilltop for the order to invade. I was ecstatic that I was succeeding in nursing, that Ori was actually gaining weight from *my* milk, despite my doubts and fears during the pregnancy. I had no energy for anyone beyond my breast.

Rubbing Ori's back, I decided to write Les later while Ori slept. I would tell him that I loved him and hoped he would take good care of himself in Lebanon, because we needed him at home. I would describe Ori's frequent smiles, the fingers that made bells ring, his miraculous mouth. I would let Les know how much I loved nursing our son, holding him on the rocking chair during the day, singing "Hush Little Baby" and cuddling him at night. I'd tell him how during the eighth week, when I was taking a shower, milk shpritzed from my nipples. He'd like that. And yes, I wanted him to come home, despite his one failed visit in July.

On that Friday afternoon when Les had dragged himself into the apartment with his M16 strapped over his back and a week's growth of beard, Ori cried when the scruffy face smelling of tank oil, dust, and cigarettes touched his.

"My little soldier," Les said.

"One in the family's enough," I said.

"That's what I love about coming home," Les said, looking beyond me. "All the loving support I get for defending this fucking country . . ."

I couldn't understand why he was calling Israel "this fucking country" if he loved it so much. He loved the army, feeling part of the macho in-group, the know-it-alls, even though he had only been in the country six years and served eighteen months as a new "older" immigrant. He knew more army slang than most of the guys who had served the full three years.

That Shabbat was a disaster—me needing attention, Les needing more, and Ori getting it all. No grandparents or aunts around to help. Friends' husbands also in Lebanon.

My only pleasure, other than Ori, came from my blooming geraniums on the roof garden, and my only support from the neighborhood shopkeepers on Bethlehem Road. During the long summer afternoons after Ori woke up from his nap, I would water the garden and then strap him into the Snugli and carry him down the sixty-four stairs to Bethlehem Road. Those afternoons were my happiest moments during that war.

First I'd cross the street to show Menachem HaLachmi how the little *fresser* was growing. Menachem handed me a rugelach, knowing I loved the chocolate-and-almond pastry. He'd stretch his hands over the counter and give Ori's cheek a little pinch. "*Ezzeh motek. Ezzeh hamud,*" he'd say.

Then I'd stop at Zion's shack, where he sold rubber bands, shoelaces, and scarves. "*Sh'yehiyeh barie*" was Zion's greeting. I wished him good health too and asked when he was retiring, since the permanent sign on the shack advertised a closeout sale. "Soon, soon," he'd say.

Igor, the bald Bulgarian butcher, was not the caring type, so I just nodded to him as we walked by. He nodded back. At least he never overcharged me when I bought a fresh chicken.

Shmulik Shem-Tov, the Tunisian laundry man, always held his iron with one hand and patted me on the shoulder with the other, asking about Les in Lebanon and wishing me good luck. His son served in the regular army, also in Lebanon. "It's no picnic, this war," he'd tell me, "even on the home front."

The Moroccan owner of the grocery store Eliahu Ben-Eli was usually too busy for more than a smile and a dill pickle. His wife, her head always covered with a pink *shmatte*, sat on the barrel, guarding the pickles. Ben-Eli's son was also fighting in Lebanon. He and his wife aged ten years during the first six weeks.

The storekeepers must have seen in my eyes that I was needy. They understood the nursing mother needed to be fed. I found love and caring on Bethlehem Road. Even Ovadia, the falafel man, who was not generous by nature, put in an extra ball when I ordered a full pita. This, too, I took as a sign of camaraderie and caring.

❧

Nobody ever knocked at the door during the war. Any knock would have made me think of the two soldiers and accompanying social worker coming to deliver bad news. So once, when I did hear a knock at five in the afternoon, I panicked. I was in the bathroom holding Ori's backside under the running faucet. I grabbed his towel and ran to the door with the baby folded over my left arm. Through the peephole I saw Schwartzkopf, our downstairs neighbor. He was a retired Egged Tours bus driver who talked about his days at the wheel as if he were Ben-Gurion himself, driving the young country to glory. Now that he was retired, Schwartzkopf spent whole afternoons cleaning his Volvo's motor on the sidewalk in front of the house. What did he care if young mothers had to walk in the street? He had been a prisoner of war in Jordan for seven months after the fall of the Old City in '48. The rest of the world could go to hell.

I opened the door. He started yelling. Ori wiggled around to see the voice.

"*Tizahari*," he shouted. "*Tizahari*. All the water from your geraniums is dripping onto my windowsill. Be careful. You think my wife likes to clean the windows every day because of your flowers?"

I couldn't believe my ears. We were in a war. My husband was fighting in Beirut. I was home alone with a new baby and this asshole was complaining about water on his windowsill? Clutching Ori even tighter, I walked past Schwartzkopf onto the shared tiled roof. Les and I had converted it into a roof garden. None of the neighbors cared. Schwartzkopf followed me outside, repeating his warning—"*Tizahari*. You and your American flowers."

With my free right hand I touched the heavy asbestos flower containers on the ledge of the roof, the ones with hot-pink and purple geraniums cascading over the sides. I turned toward him and asked him if these were the flowerpots he meant, "*Elu*? *Elu*?" I raised my voice.

He nodded.

"These? These?" I repeated, working up a steam.

He nodded again, stepping back.

"These right here? Are these the American flowers you mean, Mr. Schwartzkopf?" Ori wiggled and tried to look at this woman who twenty seconds earlier had been his loving mother.

"Yes," he said, "of course, those are the ones I'm talking about."

With my right hand, I shoved the heavy flower boxes onto the floor of the roof.

"Never again, Mr. Schwartzkopf," I screamed. "Never again will I dirty your fucking windows. Do you hear me?"

The pots had broken into jagged pieces and the flowers lay scattered and wounded on the floor of the roof, their roots still attached to the soil. Ori wailed.

"Is this what you mean, Schwartzkopf? Is this what you mean?" I yelled at him over and over.

He froze, then retreated a few steps. In the doorway he stood and stared at me. I could hear him thinking, *This is a woman at the end of her rope, a crazy woman, over the edge, holding a baby.*

After he left I didn't know if that mad woman was really me or if I had just played the role to get him off my back. Ori, crying uncontrollably, didn't seem to know either.

❧

Four months after he had gone off to volunteer for the war, Les called one morning at nine—during Ori's second feeding. He was in Kiryat Shmona, eating a schnitzel that the Moroccan women of the town prepared for the soldiers going in and out of Lebanon. Soon he would be getting a ride to Tel HaShomer to get his release papers. Then he'd come home. For good. Did I want to come pick him up?

Something in his voice sounded pathetic, ashamed, vanquished. The last thing I wanted to do was drive down to Tel HaShomer Hospital near Tel Aviv in the heat, with Ori in the back seat. For weeks I had avoided fixing the air conditioning in the car. I wasn't about to rush to do it that morning and then drive down there.

When I didn't jump at the opportunity, Les understood.

"No more Lebanon," he said, his voice half dead.

I felt sorry for him, for what he had been through—though I didn't know what he had been through—and for my lack of response to his call for help. He sounded tired, exhausted, but so was I.

As always when he called, other soldiers were clamoring around him to use the phone. I heard him swear at them to shut up so he could hear me.

"Are you happy I'm coming home?"

This was so out of character. He never asked if I was happy about anything. "Of course," I said. It was partially true. At times I did miss him. I was glad he was finally out of physical danger, or would be soon. Driving anywhere in Lebanon became more dangerous the longer we stayed. Twelve-year-old boys were shooting rocket propelled grenades at Israeli convoys. But during my husband's four-month absence, I had gotten used to full-time, on-demand nursing. I was apprehensive of any change in my nonroutine routine.

All day I straightened up the house, making sure the toilet bowls sparkled, the sinks shone. Ori followed me around on his knees, giving me quizzical looks, as if to say, *Who is this woman cleaning the house?*

By the evening news, Les still hadn't arrived and hadn't called. I sat down with Ori in the rocking chair in the living room. While I burped him, I sang our favorite lullaby.

Hush little baby, don't say a word
Papa's gonna buy you a mockingbird.

As soon as he was asleep on my shoulder, there was a knock on the door. Ori twitched but didn't wake up. I carried him to the entrance hall, his head resting on my shoulder, and opened the door.

Les stood there, unshaven, wearing a wrinkled plaid shirt opened at the chest and green army pants filthy with dust and grease. Around his neck hung his silver dog tag chain, the tag itself hidden by his shirt. His army knapsack was strung over one shoulder, and over the other he carried an M16. He stood surrounded by a heavy silence, dazed, staring at the Hebrew sign on the door with our names on it, as if there were no relationship between those names and this house.

In his right hand he held a single red rose. Eventually he extended his right arm and handed me the flower. I took it with my free hand. For a moment we held the rose together, our eyes locked. Then he let go and I drew the bud to my nose. The smell was familiar and reminded me of places a million miles from Beirut, from Jerusalem, from the whole warring Middle East. I had grown up in such a place.

"Just a minute." I turned around to take Ori to his own room for the first time in four months. I put the rose down on the changing table and then I laid Ori down gently in his bed, so he wouldn't wake up and balk.

Les hadn't moved. He stood there, waiting. "Come," I said, opening my arms. "Welcome home."

He walked past me slowly, laid down his weapon and knapsack in the entrance hall.

I lowered my arms.

Bare, he seemed to lose his balance for a second, but then he cleared his throat and flattened his mustache over his lips with his thumb and forefinger. My husband was home, for good.

"Thank you," I said.

"For what?"

"The rose. You." I opened my arms again. He fell into them. We stood there in the entrance hall for a long time, me holding him, he too tired or dazed or who knows what to hug me back. The longer we stood there in this unbalanced embrace, the heavier he felt. It occurred to me that he might fall asleep in this position.

"What's to eat?" he said finally, voicing these words by rote.

I had made a special goulash for his homecoming. He sat down at the head of the dining table and seemed pleased to be served. He touched my hand when I put the full warm plate in front of him. I bent down and kissed his forehead.

It smelled of sweat and cedar.

After dinner he went into the bathroom and stayed. For hours. Before I went to bed at eleven, I knocked on the bathroom door.

"Don't do that," he clipped.

"Do what?"

"Knock."

"I did knock."

"Don't do that," he said, raising his voice.

I had had fantasies of our first night together, after passionate kissing and love-making, staying up to talk about our Ori, his war.

I don't know when he came to bed, but when he did, I heard an unfamiliar moan and heavy breathing. His crawling into our bed sounded like a military operation, some camouflage maneuver.

When Ori awoke at three thirty to nurse, I went to him with eyes half-open and carried him to the rocking chair in the living room. We sat there for an hour, dozing, nursing, and singing.

If that diamond ring turns brass
Papa's gonna buy you a looking glass.
I slowed down and sang softer.
If that looking glass gets broke,
Papa's gonna buy you a billy goat.

After each verse, I felt a deep sadness pulling at me from inside.

If that billy goat don't pull
Papa's gonna buy you a cart and bull.

It was a sadness like no other, a feeling of total devastation and loss.

If that cart and bull turn over,
Papa's gonna buy you a dog named Rover.
By the last verse, my tears flowed like milk.
If that dog named Rover don't bark,

Papa's gonna buy you a horse and cart.

The last lines were barely audible.

And if that horse and cart fall
down,
You'll still
be
the sweetest
little
ba-by
in
town.

I pulled Ori tighter to my chest. The moon made frightening shadows on the living room walls, shadows that reminded me of soldiers hiding behind closed doors and large men dressed in black brandishing swords.

Then I thought of the hug I had given Les in the entrance hall and how he couldn't hug back, how he hid in the bathroom the whole night. I wondered what he had done in Lebanon. I wanted him to tell me and to hug me like before the war. These thoughts and memories filled me with longing and sadness.

The next morning Les sat on the edge of the bed and stared at his paratroop boots.

"They need polishing," he said softly. It wasn't clear if he was asking me to polish them or just stating a fact. "I have to go back to Tel HaShomer." His voice was an eerie monotone.

"Why?" I asked, sitting on the edge next to him.

"To return all the equipment. I didn't finish yesterday." He looked at his feet as he spoke, his tone torpid.

He was tired, said he hadn't slept the whole night, wished I wouldn't sing to the baby in the middle of the night. It kept him up.

I tried to give him a hug, but it felt like I was hugging all the men in his armored troop carrier, as if Les were carrying all those who had survived and those who had been killed, carrying them all with their flak jackets and weapons and helmets in his stiff body. There was no soft place for me.

We fell into a pattern. Every night after I put Ori to sleep, I washed dishes and he read the paper. At nine, we watched the news, Les gritting his teeth and cursing every time Arik Sharon appeared on-screen. Then we read more newspapers, each ensconced in our black-and-white tents. At eleven I went to sleep and he went into the bathroom. At two or three he'd come to bed. One night when I was coming back from nursing Ori and he was just getting into bed, I leaned over to him and whispered in his ear. He brushed me away as if I were a mosquito.

"Don't do that," he snapped. I touched him gently. Slowly we started to make love, but as soon as my breathing became strong, he pushed me away. "Enough," he said. "Never make those sounds in my ear."

One Shabbat afternoon in November of '82, Ori and I were playing peekaboo on the living room floor. Les snuck into the living room from the roof with a piece of the hose I used to water the few flower survivors from the Schwartzkopf incident. Les had cut off a foot-long piece and was holding it on his right shoulder.

"Be careful," he whispered, ducking under the dining room table.

Ori looked at him and started to laugh. I was happy Les was joining in our play.

"Quiet," Les yelled. With his left hand he aimed the pretend M16 all over the living room. "Bang. Boom," he shouted. "I'm going to kill you."

Then from his nose and throat he made noises like a wild boar. He held the hose still and aimed it at us.

Ori's laugh turned to a cry. I picked him up and we crawled and crouched behind the couch.

"Abba's playing war," I said. I patted his head and started humming "Hush Little Baby." Then, reaching over the couch, I pointed my forefinger at Les and said, "Bang, bang."

"Shut the fuck up," Les shouted.

I peeked to look at him. He was lying on his stomach, looking through the hose and taking aim.

"I see you," he said. "Bang."

"Peekaboo," I said, but by now Ori was crying louder and clutching my neck.

"It's just a game," I said, fear crouching next to me.

"Make him shut up," Les yelled. "Make him shut the fuck up." Then Les crawled out from under the table and stood up. I was afraid he was going to walk toward us and throw the hose at us, but he threw it on the floor and ran out of the house, cursing so all the neighbors could hear, "Goddamned son of a bitch, why isn't there anything to eat in this fucking house!"

I held on to Ori as hard as I could. I wanted to be sure his abba wasn't coming back with something more dangerous than a hose.

My voice withdrawn and taut, I sang, "You'll still be the sweetest little baby in town."

After a few minutes of silence, we stood up. I carried Ori out to the roof garden. Was Les there, or had he gone downstairs, taken the car?

I stood at the edge, clutching Ori, and looked down onto Bethlehem Road. The car was still parked across the street in front of Menachem's bakery. When I raised my eyes, I saw Les standing behind an electric pole near the curb. He seemed to be carving something into the pole, either with a pen or a penknife, but it didn't work. He threw his implement into the street. He flattened his body against the pole, peeking out every now and then from either side, looking up at the roof, to the left and to the right, checking to see from where the fire—or salvation—might come. I looked straight at him, but he didn't acknowledge me. He wrapped both arms around the pole and started heaving. The terrifying sound of his moans reached the roof. Part of me wanted to go hide in the living room and lock the door. Another part wanted to race down the stairs and put my arms around my husband, push my body into his, hug the pole with him, and then turn him around and direct his head to my chest; I wanted to hold his head in my hands and tell him it would be all right, that everything would be all right, the war was over, I would take care of him, we would find our love, we could do this; *I can save you*, I wanted to say, and as I imagined the words I would tell him, Ori started crying, now from hunger mixed with fear, and Les unraveled himself from the electric pole and, with his arms dangling at his sides like dead branches, started walking away down Bethlehem Road, toward Zion, Ovadia, Igor, and Ben-Eli, and I wondered if the war was still going on in their homes too and how long it would take to end.

DISPERSION

*. . . for the days of your slaughter
and your dispersions have come . . .*

JEREMIAH 25:34

41 BETHLEHEM ROAD

INVENTORY

There is no moonlight.

Of course. The First of Elul, cooler evenings, shorter days, and now this "*Rachamim, Rachamim,*" the neighbor's friend calling to him at four in the morning, each syllable rising by a half note, creating a plaintive cry slitting the night, piercing her sleep like an oud, strumming on the din of normalcy. She lies in bed, eyes slit-opened, dozing in the liminal space between darkness and dawn. The three syllables, *Ra-cha-mim,* ascend from the earth three stories below, enter the dark bedroom through the open porch doors, and hover over Nimrod's armored body.

Rachamim, not only the name of the wobbly Moroccan man who lives downstairs but also the word for "compassion." And a synonym for her name: Nechama. She lies still on her back, lips and larynx juggling the three syllables. An ambivalent haze hovers over the bed. During the past weeks she has been so preoccupied with her own inner timing that she forgot the holidays are only a month away. The holidays—food, family togetherness, food, new clothes, stress, food. She has hardly given them any thought, so focused has she been on *after* the holidays, *after* the holiday vacation, when Rafael and Aya will return to school and she will move to an apartment across the street.

How will she survive the holidays? She prefers not to think about it, not now. Now she is playing with the *Ra-cha-mim*, repeating its lilt to herself until it almost brings tears. In previous years these middle-of-the-night wake-up calls angered her. Why couldn't the friend knock on Rachamim's door? Why did he have to wake up the neighborhood, like a town crier? But this year Nechama is not angry. Now, surveying her silent room (save for Nimrod's light snoring and the occasional buzz of the mosquito zapper from the hallway), this year the word lands in an unexplored region of her psyche, a locale dense and unfathomable as the moon. "Beyond anger," she names it.

Nechama draws the lightweight cotton blanket up to her neck, opens her eyes fully, and sits up against the headboard. She pulls her hair behind her ears and twists it into a knot. On the wall opposite her, above the top shelf of the white bookshelves, hangs the enlarged photo of Rafael and Aya when they were four and two. Their smiles, as if aimed at her, make her sad. She recalls the day she took them downtown by bus to the photographer's to be photographed for their father's thirty-fifth birthday. Two weeks later the children's photograph hung in the store's front window. It stayed there almost a year. How surprised she had been when her friends called to say they saw Rafi and Aya downtown. "Model children," one said; "model family," another.

She'd had no idea the photographer would use the photo for his own publicity, but she didn't mind. In fact, she was flattered that he thought her children were model material.

Now, as she looks at Rafi and Aya when they were younger, she sees a hint of an exemplary duo, Rafi's left arm embracing his little sister—OK, so four fingers on his right hand are clenched— Aya, an open-mouth smile full of playfulness, clinging to the neck of her adored older brother, in her right hand beneath his ear that gold bell the photographer handed her at the last minute to ensure smiles. In another second, she will bite her brother's cheek and he will hit her, but in this one frame, joy.

Fourteen years. The little boy's fist now usually closed, no longer that little girl's anchor. Nechama takes a deep breath and lets go of the photo. She will take it with her.

She follows the top shelf of the bookshelves to the right, where three bottles of perfume stand in a line. She purchased each one at the duty-free on her last three trips to her father. Why did she buy them? Who did she want to smell good for? The dark-green bottle is shaped like a heart. Two glass ridges border the name: Tender Poison. Ah, yes, that's why she bought it, for its name. She used that perfume the few times she and Nimrod went to a movie. "The smell is disgusting," he'd said, and told her to get rid of it. Yes, she will take the small bottle with her and leave the other two for Aya.

The perfumes sit next to the silk jewelry box from her mother, who bought it on her trip to China. The silk is out of place in an apartment where everything is stone, marble, glass, or wood. She will slip her wedding ring into the box and take it with her.

At the end of the shelf, a clear plastic file leans against the corner wall. Inside are Aunt Betty's photocopies of her English translation of a great aunt's letters in Hungarian. Nechama read the letters years ago when they arrived but could not get excited about a woman who made candles in some unpronounceable village in eastern Hungary in 1924. So why keep them? She doesn't know why, but she will take them with her to the apartment across the street.

Surveying her belongings helps her choose who she will become across the street, what she chooses to remember, what she chooses to forget, and what she will leave behind. She likes this spontaneous early morning inventory and whispers a thank-you to Rachamim's friend for the wake-up call.

The eerie yellow numbers on the clock next to her side of the bed show 4:05 a.m. She will definitely take the clock with her, with its two AA batteries. After all, it is hers. She bought it at Avrami's store the morning she decided she deserved her own clock. Why should she have to sit halfway up in bed balanced on her elbow, twist, and stretch over Nimrod's body whenever she wanted to see the time? What a fool she had been.

A wave of cool air comes in through the porch doors, different than the Av air two weeks ago. More moisture now, when God has compassion on the citizens of hot, dry Jerusalem and shows it in Elul by sending whispers of longed-for rain. Nechama can already smell her future, the relief to be out of the house.

She needs transitions, those periods of time that break behaviors stuck in one place. Transitions offer hope, change. She will always partner Elul with *Ra-cha-mim*, no matter where she lives. Yet, as this thought passes through her mind, she feels her stomach tighten. Her gut is more aware of a certain sadness brought on by the season. Elul. Fall.

She is relieved, knowing she has a contract for an apartment across the street. The kids will be able to come over whenever they want. There's an extra bedroom or two, if they want to stay the night with her, or move in. Being so close will make her leaving easier on everyone.

She pulls up the blanket to cover her mouth. Its edge gives off a faint smell of sunshine. She dries all her laundry on the roof porch. The new place does not have a roof porch, but it has windows and a small narrow porch that faces Rehov Levi. She inhales deeply; she will take this smell with her. She grins at her decision but knows this is a smile on the verge of desolation. She strains to convince herself: there will always be sunlight, no matter where she lives.

A door slams downstairs. The two men are muttering in loud whispers that become fainter as they move away from the door. She imagines Rachamim and his friend crossing Bethlehem Road, empty in the middle of the night. This image causes a disproportionate sadness. Rachamim, her downstairs neighbor for twenty-three years, has never let Rafael and Aya play in the backyard, even though the backyard is common property.

Soon the men will walk into Tikvatenu, their little Moroccan synagogue on Zerubavel Alley. Rachamim will turn on the light and wait for the *minyan* to form. Then they will begin to chant the Elul prayers for forgiveness in their synagogue the size of a one-car garage. *Tikvatenu, Our Hope.*

Nimrod's body heaves with each breath. He sleeps with no covers and no clothes. Nechama likes nightgowns, bathrobes, blankets. She will take the purple knit blanket, a hand-me-down from her aunt. The edges have been frayed since the day she received it and the satin edging is falling off, but still, it is a wonderful blanket and she is glad to cover herself with something from her loving aunt. It will get her through the "after the holidays" season.

There are so many details to consider. Maybe she will start making lists, though seeing the minute details of her life on paper gives her leaving—no, it isn't a leaving, it is just moving across the street—a certain permanency.

Maybe something will happen during Elul or the holidays that will change everything. Maybe Nimrod will apologize for his verbal abuse or go abroad for a few months or die. Then she will stay in her beloved home with her beloved children.

Which sheets will she take with her? Which cutlery? The serving spoons? Will Nimrod agree to her taking the two-volume English-Hebrew dictionary, or will he insist on splitting it, as he did the four-volume *Archaeology of the Bible*?

"It is just a trial," she told him, when she first mentioned the idea of separation in Tamuz. She doesn't use the d-word. She doesn't want to fracture the family. She can't bear that thought. She just needs time. Alone.

He laughed, as if she were talking gibberish. "Trial, shmial," he said. Rarely does he take anything she says seriously. Usually she gives in, but not now. After twenty-four years of marriage, she feels sure of herself. Nothing will make her change her mind. She cannot become who she needs to be in the same house with him. She needs to hear her own voice, not his barbaric yawp.

He thinks she is crazy and selfish and tells her so every day. "You let food turn blue in the fridge. You don't hang up the children's towels. All you do is think of yourself."

"Is it selfish to learn to like yourself?" she asks him.

He laughs.

"I will only be moving across the street," she says, still defensive. "The kids can stay with me, if they want."

He slams doors, calls her names—"idiot," "dumb cunt."

She stood outside the bathroom door and explained that if there were a rental in the same building, she would move downstairs. "Let's not make a big deal out of it," she said. "Just a temporary separation."

But as the date of her departure approached, she started daring to imagine her move as permanent. She hoped Rafael and Aya would visit her, even sleep over, but she couldn't be sure. In any case, ever since she told them the plan, they had been spending more time at their friends' houses than at their own.

She glances at Nimrod sleeping and slides quietly out of bed, her bare feet in her slippers, the pink ones with the fur around the ankles. They give her a sense of stability. She grabs her terry cloth robe from the back of the bedroom door and walks into the hallway. The door to Rafael's room is closed. She walks through the entrance hall to look in on Aya, but her door is closed as well. She wraps herself in her robe, walks into the living room, and sits on the TV chair. It is still depressed from Nimrod's evening sitting.

The two windows facing the street are wide open to let in the cool night air. Prayers of forgiveness drift up into the living room from Tikvatenu. She closes her eyes and joins the *minyan* by proxy, first asking, then pleading with God for forgiveness, moving into that plaintive space.

After a minute she opens her eyes and surveys the room. She doesn't look at the books or the TV on the wall unit but the shelves themselves. She and Nimrod painted them during their first year of marriage. The shelves were made from the lift that her father had sent from Pittsburgh. Nimrod borrowed an electric saw and converted the lift into shelves. They sanded and painted together, arguing only about the color. Now the shelves are full of bric-a-brac collected from trips to New Mexico, Italy, and Greece. He can keep all that. Nor does she want the television or the B&O stereo with its enormous speakers.

Above the shelves hangs the paper cutting that her mother gave them for their first anniversary. In the half darkness of the room, Nechama traces the outline of the old man lifting his hands toward heaven while the words of the psalm encircle him: *If I forget thee oh Jerusalem, let my . . .* The punishment for forgetting is too horrible.

Why did the psalmist choose such an awful curse? She swivels around in the chair toward the open window. How much must one remember the city? A husband? How much must one sacrifice? Does she need to devote all her emotional energy to remembering Jerusalem?

Nechama will leave the paper cutting in place, above the television. Without it, the wall, or perhaps the entire room, or even all the inhabitants, will lose their moorings. She has the psalm inside her.

Now she swivels toward the north wall. Here is a watercolor of a brown door, slightly ajar. She insisted on placing the painting there, opposite the entrance door to the apartment and catty-corner to the porch door. She is amazed at how many doors she needs in her life. The painting is Nimrod's, but the position is hers. She will leave it in place.

Swiveling again, she focuses on the narrow southern wall where two sand drawings from New Mexico hang. She and Nimrod bought them on a trip to Las Cruces, where a Navaho woman asked her why her husband takes so many pictures. When Nechama asked him, he said, "What kind of stupid question is that?" She wants one sand drawing. It will remind her of possibilities she experienced in New Mexico.

The dining table stands firm and secure next to the cabinets that divide the kitchen from the living space. Made of cherrywood in an ellipsis shape, the table commands six chairs around it. Nechama reupholstered the chairs last year. She is happy with the choice of the woven rose fabric that doesn't show stains or dust, but Nimrod doesn't like the color. This table is the scene of their Friday-night meals, the only time the family eats together, now that the kids are in high school. Of course it will stay, along with the chairs.

Looking outside, she sees stars in the western sky. They know their place. She will always have stars, even across the street. On the chipped white coffee table sits a blue metal platter, layered, cut with a laser. She bought it at the annual Hutzot HaYotzer Crafts Fair, where she goes every year, alone. She likes to arrange fresh fruit on its different layers. It is hers. She chose it and will definitely take it with her. The hanging lamp fixture she will not touch, nor the expensive intaglio they bought before the children were born on a once-in-a-lifetime art spree in Tel Aviv. She loves its circular image, a sunset in brown, magenta, peach, and mustard hues, encircled by a line from Psalms. She can conjure this piece at will when she closes her eyes, no matter where she lives. This is enough.

A loud wail, like a jackal, startles her. It takes her a moment to realize it is the shofar from Tikvatenu. Of course, the sound that opens God's ears and man's tongue. Forgiveness. Compassion. Repentance.

She needs very little, in actuality, for she has memorized this room—its furniture, light fixtures, and decorative pieces—just as she has memorized every other room in the house. They are inside her. Wherever she roams, she will carry the rooms of her home with her. Though soon, she will no longer live inside them.

A hand rests on her shoulder. She tenses and turns around. Nimrod stands, naked.

"Who was knocking?" he asks, on the verge of reprimanding.

She lifts her other shoulder and shakes her head.

"Why are you here?" he says, standing over her, rubbing his face and chest with his free open palm.

"I want to hear the shofar," she lies. "You heard it?"

"I'm not deaf, you know," he counters. "Give me *some* credit." After a short silence, he puts his hand gently on her head. He did this once before, on their first date, when they saw *Bonnie and Clyde* in a Jerusalem movie theater. They laughed together when young men in the audience rolled their empty pop bottles down the cold cement floor. But then Nimrod swore at them and almost started a fistfight. All she remembers about the movie is the sound of rolling glass on cement and the palm of his hand on her head.

"Don't leave," he whispers.

The words hang in the night air; they seek refuge in her heart.

Nechama knows how hard it is for her husband to say these words. She closes her eyes and wonders. Is this the change she's been waiting for? The change she has longed for, for so many lonely years?

She sits in silence, thinking about this man, her husband, the life they've built together in this space over twenty-four years, their children, their only home. Suddenly, with her inner eye, she sees an iron door falling from the sky. It descends slowly and then picks up speed as it approaches Bethlehem Road. The door falls like a meteor toward their living room. If she does not leave, she will be crushed.

Nechama opens her eyes to avoid catastrophe. Nimrod turns and walks slowly back to their bed. She sees scratches on his upper back from the last time they made love. They look like letters in search of words.

These, too, Nechama will take with her.

Avrami, Home Building Supplies

On Shabbat I'm going to drive down to Arad to bring my grandson up to Jerusalem. I want to show him the Wailing Wall and all the new sites. I live for this kid. Last Shabbat he said, "Saba, take me to Ree-shalem." Isn't that the cutest thing you've ever heard? Reeshalem! I said, "Sure, sweetie, for you Saba will do anything. Next week I will take you to Reeshalem and we will see the Wailing Wall."

No, he tells me, he doesn't want to see the Wailing Wall and I say why and he says because I'm a big boy now and I don't cry anymore. Couldn't you die? I'm a big boy now and I don't cry. He's only four and a half. Yitzhak Shalom, named after my father, may his soul rest in peace, killed by that bastard, may his name be erased forever. What he did to us Jews in Romania, you don't want to know. Don't ask.

Now we're hoping for a little girl so she can have my mother's name, Channa Rivka.

I'm sorry. I always get a little teary when I talk about the family. How many nails did you say you need? I'll tell my wife to wrap a few in some old newspaper. She's back there. Do you see her? Drinking her tea. She cries all the time. As if it all happened last week. But it's twenty-five years. Good that she comes to help me in the store. Otherwise, I'd have a basket case on my hands.

Here, take a lollipop for your little girl.

MALKA'S HOLOCAUST

Malka has painted her lips Root Red for today's ceremony.

"Why get *farputzt*?" asks Yudit, her only friend at Beit Avraham. "The dead see?"

It's 9:58 a.m. and the two women are standing in front of their orange plastic chairs in the back row of the culture hall, along with the other 118 old Jews from central Europe. In two minutes, sirens will call all Israelis to stand silent and still for 120 seconds and remember the six million.

Malka's eyes are watering. "It's the Memoir Lady," she whispers to Yudit. Then Malka hums "Ave Maria."

Yudit gives her a gentle poke in the ribs with her good elbow. "Shhh," she exhales. "Time for the blast."

The siren begins its terrible shriek. Malka lowers her head. This year it sounds like a band of a thousand wailing shofars, all off-key. *Remember me*, they beseech. *Remember me.* Malka closes her eyes and, in the darkness, tries to find her father, the way he looked the last time she saw him. She can't remember; she wants to kill Edith, the Memoir Lady.

For the past eight months, this Edith has been turning Malka's official afternoon *Schlafstunde* into a nightmare.

"What the hell is memoir?" Malka had protested to Lily, her daughter, who cooked up the scheme, just as she had instigated Malka's move from Tel Aviv to Beit Avraham.

"Think of Tomer and Nofit, Ema. It's important they know what happened to their grandma during the Holocaust." Lily made her mother promise to call Edith for an appointment.

Malka called. Edith, a woman two heads taller than Malka who never wore lipstick, appeared one afternoon in September fully equipped with a portable tape recorder. "Audio cassette," Edith said proudly. "You say any memory into this little miracle, and it will store it," she bragged. "Or restore it."

"Where?" Malka asked, poking a few buttons. A lid flipped open and out jumped a tape.

"That's the cassette," Edith said. "It's magnetic and stores everything you say about the war after you push RECORD and start talking." Malka put on her glasses to read the small print. "When you press REWIND and then PLAY, you'll hear your memories." In case Malka didn't feel comfortable with the machine, Edith suggested paper and a felt-tip pen.

Edith also came with a list of stupid questions in German, Hebrew, and Dutch: What was it like being in hiding? Did you miss your family? What was the best part of "being" Catholic?

"These are your memoir tools," Edith said on that first Thursday in September, fifty years after the war ended.

Standing now in the back row of the culture hall of Beit Avraham, Malka is sorry she agreed to the whole megillah. The device was invasive. She had lived fine without Frans for five decades. What business was it of Edith's to dredge up the past? Why hadn't she, Malka, stood up to her manipulative daughter and said no? No more Holocaust. If the grandchildren want Holocaust, let them go to Poland with their classmates and go shopping the last day. Isn't that why the kids joined those ridiculous trips?

When the siren gains momentum, aiming to crack the earth's crust, Shaul Schwartzman in the front row coughs. Happens every year. His raspy cough has become part of the performance, familiar as the siren itself, familiar as Chaya Rubinstein's sobs from the other end of the back row.

During the first month, Malka wrote with the felt-tip pen and cut out photos from her photo album with her sewing scissors. She glued a headshot of her mother onto a clean page while she remembered the family piano in Amsterdam. Edith approved, but she preferred the machine, so by mid-February Malka befriended the tape recorder. By the end of June the family would have a desktop-published booklet, replete with (edited) verbatim memories, photos, maps, names, numbers, the works—an authentic Dutch Holocaust story, five traumatic years reduced to fifty pages, double-spaced, 14-point type, Century Gothic.

Neither Schwartzman's cough nor Rubinstein's cry takes Malka away from her beloved "Ave Maria! Jungfrau mild . . ."

Ave Maria! maiden mild!
Listen to a maiden's prayer!
Thou canst hear though from the wild;
Thou canst save amid despair.
Safe may we sleep beneath thy care,
Though banish'd, outcast and reviled—
Maiden! hear a maiden's prayer;
Mother, hear a suppliant child!

Frans had taught her the words as he played it on the piano in the parlor. Malka hums as the siren reaches its crescendo. Shaul and Chaya with their Mengele Holocaust would be horrified, are horrified. Hasn't Malka seen it in their eyes whenever Malka's Holocaust comes up at five o'clock tea during the weeks preceding Holocaust Remembrance Day?

Anyone who didn't experience at least one rat-infested labor camp, one concentration camp, one death march, one year in a typhus-rampant ghetto, even six months in a stinking cowshed—how can you call that a Holocaust?

The women at Beit Avraham who moved to Palestine from Europe in the 1920s or '30s know not to even come down for tea in the weeks before Holocaust Remembrance Day. How can they understand what happened in Europe, dancing, as they did, in the fields of the Jezreel Valley under full moons, or hiding from Arab marauders in Jerusalem? Only a few Jews were killed then. No torture, even. No gas.

But today, fifty years after her charade ended, Malka is tired of being ashamed of her past. Enough. She has apologized enough. It is not her fault her father was smart enough to send her into hiding earlier than most Dutch Jews. She is sick of apologizing for her comforts during the war. Enough! For how long does she have to say, "Sorry for not having numbers tattooed on my arm"? Enough! Isn't it enough she lost her parents and brother?

This "Enough" business is the only good thing Edith the Memoir Lady has done for her. And the audio cassette player. Edith pushed Malka to reclaim exact dates and names, descriptions and feelings. "You won't fall apart if you describe Klara Korteweg," Edith said. So Malka described. The flat tasteless wafers on her tongue. The sour wine on her lips. The strange smell of liquor in church. The priest's meaty hands. Malka's wish for a miracle. If a virgin gave birth and a few fish fed thousands, why couldn't her parents and brother appear at the front door of the

Kortewegs' house in Vught, thank the generous couple for hiding their Malki, and take her back to Amsterdam?

The siren ends. A silence heavy as an elephant presses on the culture hall for seven elongated seconds, after which all 120 residents start *futzling* in their pockets for tissues and turn around to make sure their orange plastic chairs have not levitated during the scream. Squirming like passengers on an overcrowded train, they wiggle to find comfortable positions.

Malka recalls the chair in the Kortewegs' parlor that Edith asked her to describe. It was dark-brown leather with gold pins under the rounded heavy arms. Cornelis sat there in the evenings, smoking his pipe, reading his newspaper, while Mrs. Korteweg sat on the couch, cutting scraps of cotton fabric for her quilts. Malka sat at the dark wooden desk doing her algebra.

This was the room where she first saw Frans, though she had *heard* him first. That afternoon in the kitchen with Mrs. Korteweg ("You never called her Klara?" Edith asked). They were about to spoon Mrs. Korteweg's plum jam into jars, pour on the paraffin, seal the jars, and take them to the shed for storage. Thirty-two jars were lined up in four rows on the wooden kitchen table. It was September 1943. The window was open slightly, letting in a lovely fall breeze that reminded Malka of home.

Mrs. Korteweg hovered over her. "Maria, we mustn't have any hairs in the jam. Go to your room and put a net over your hair."

Malka opened the heavy wooden kitchen door and walked down the long hallway toward the staircase leading up to the bedrooms. At the foot of the staircase, she stopped. Someone was in the parlor playing the piano. The door was closed.

The residents look at their watches, checking if the siren lasted the full 120 seconds. Malka hears a generic kvetch moving through the culture hall, as if a choir of central European Jews, mostly female, sighs *oy* and *feh* pianissimo.

The director of Beit Avraham stands in front of the audience. He is a retired Israel Defense Forces general. The residents are his privates and the staff his officers. He begins his annual speech about how the residents must pass on the legacy of the Holocaust to their grandchildren and great-grandchildren.

"I can't even remember what I ate for dinner last night," Yudit whispers to Malka.

"I should be so lucky to have great-grandchildren," Malka says. "Nobody wants to marry anymore." They are both shushed by Batsheva, who turns around from the row in front of them, putting her forefinger to her lips; Batsheva, who survived Treblinka and walked barefoot to Israel through snow and heat, through Turkey, Syria, and Lebanon, carrying her infirm three-year-old daughter on her back, a mythic journey that took two years and aged her by ten; Batsheva, who supports the director's every word.

"We have an example right here this morning," the director continues. He lifts his hand, and Subhi, one of the Arab men from maintenance, rolls the piano to the front of the room. The director points to the eldest grandson of Shaul Schwartzman and invites him to come play.

Malka stretches her neck to see, but this causes a pain in her left shoulder blade.

"Like all Jewish holidays," Yudit whispers. "Tears first; then song."

Malka is grateful she has found one of the few women in Beit Avraham who did not experience a death camp, a pile of corpses on top of her body in a pit, or a snowy death march. She is also grateful that Yudit did not spend the war years in Palestine and thus does not romanticize secret Hagana meetings, handsome, dead Palmach leaders, folk dancing under full moons. She is grateful Yudit likes *mit Schlag* and still reads German newspapers, that she talks about Fifth Avenue and the Brooklyn Bridge, that she lived in New York from '37 to '49 because her father got her family out of Vienna in time.

Yudit nudges Malka. "If yours was the five-star Holocaust, Malki, mine was the deluxe. No hunger. No hiding. No gas."

"No Holocaust," Malka says, and they lower their heads to giggle.

"Now Yitzchak Schwartzman, a student at the Rubin Academy," the director says with martial authority, "named after his great-grandfather, the musician Yitzchak Schwartzman of blessed memory *ben* Chaya and Mottel, from the town of Łódź, who perished in the gas chamber at Auschwitz two months before the end of the war, will play some of the *Lieder* that his great-grandfather loved so well."

Malka tries again to stretch her neck, this time to the right. She succeeds with no pain.

"Our own Shaul Schwartzman has told us often how he remembers the last time he saw his beloved father singing those German *Lieder* as he marched into the showers at Auschwitz." The director nods toward the elder Schwartzman, who nods in affirmation, as if saying, *Yes, it was a terrible memory and now it is soldered into my brain and I will never let it go.*

"What poetic justice to hear these songs here and now in the security of Beit Avraham, in the united city of Jerusalem, the eternal capital of the Jewish People, in the sovereign and democratic State of Israel . . . forever and ever."

Arthritic hands clap.

"He forgot 'holy,'" says Yudit.

"May we commemorate many Holocaust Remembrance Days together," concludes the director.

"*Ad me'ah v'esrim*," Malka says under her breath.

"Only 120?" Yudit whispers back.

Malka watches the young Schwartzman walk toward the piano, his eyes fixed to the windows through which the pines stand tall as guards in the warm April morning. The young Schwartzman is tall, too, but pale and thin. He could use more schnitzel. He stands in front of the piano and turns toward the old people, some with plastic pipes coming out of their noses. His eyes are a soft gray that match his gray plaid shirt. "*Parveh*," Malka whispers into Yudit's good ear. The young Schwartzman offers a shy smile and a half-bow. He looks left and right. Maybe he had prepared a short speech, but among the breathing archaeological remains, the boy has forgotten his words. He lowers himself onto the piano bench. His gentle eyes bore into the keys, as if he is looking beyond and beneath the ivory, and he begins.

Schubert. "Gute Nacht." Malka cups her hands over her mouth. She smells the lipstick on her fingers. It reminds her of sweet plums. "Gute Nacht," the first song of *Winterreise*. Though she knows it is improper to hum during concerts, hum she does, ignoring Yudit's gentle nudge and the director's less gentle stare.

The music was so beautiful. Malka stood behind the closed door at the foot of the staircase. Who was playing in the middle of the afternoon? Cornelis wasn't home yet and he was the only one who ever touched the piano in the parlor. "Der Lindenbaum," one of Malka's favorite Schubert *Lieder*. She had learned the song in school during her last year in Amsterdam. Her mother sometimes played it on their piano at home. She leaned against the door and sang the words softly to herself.

Am Brunnen vor dem Tore
Da steht ein Lindenbaum:
Ich träumt in seinem Schatten
So manchen süßen Traum.
By the well before the gate
there stands a linden tree.
I dreamed in its shadow
some sweet dreams.

A man was singing. She closed her eyes. Her chest began to heave.

After a few minutes Mrs. Korteweg walked down the long corridor from the kitchen and found Malka leaning against the door.

"Move on, Maria," she scolded in a whisper. "Get on your net. Plums a-waiting."

Later, in the kitchen, while the two stood and poured the fresh jam into the jars, Malka asked Mrs. Korteweg who was playing.

"A soldier," she said, as if this information were not important.

Malka stopped working and held the edge of the table. "What kind of soldier?"

"A wounded one, Maria."

"What . . ."

Before Malka could finish her question, Mrs. Korteweg explained that the young man was a Dutch volunteer in the Totenkopf Division of the Waffen SS.

Malka collapsed onto the nearest chair. "The SS?"

"He's convalescing in the government home. Two kilometers down the road, bless his soul. May Mother Mary watch over him. Such a sweet fellow."

Malka tapped her fingers on the wooden table so Mrs. Korteweg would not hear her pounding heart.

"I know the nurse at the home, a good Catholic. She knows we have a piano and asked if he could practice. He's very bored, poor soul. Not yet healed."

Thoughts raced through Malka's mind. "What kind of soldier?" she repeated.

"I think it's the 34.SS Freiwilligen Grenadier Division. Is that better, Maria? Can you please stand up and help me pour all this jam? We need to cover it up."

Malka wondered if Mrs. Korteweg had agreed to have the wounded soldier come to her house so he would uncover Malka's secret. If not, why would she take the risk? How wounded could he be if he walked the two kilometers to play the piano? Was she trying to get her caught? But that didn't make sense. If Malka were caught, the Kortewegs would be sent to jail. Or worse.

"I want to meet him," Malka said. She remembered what her father had told her the day he took her to the train station in Amsterdam. It was snowing. The sky was dark gray, ominous. The woman from the underground had just arrived. Malka wondered if she would ever see her father again.

Remember this, Malki: All German soldiers are stupid. Then he kissed her goodbye.

She believed him, like she believed everything else he had said that day.

We will meet as soon as possible. If not during the war, then after. We will all survive—you, your brother, Mamma, and I. We are smarter than they are.

She was fourteen. She promised to remember everything her father told her, but if she learned anything living as Maria with Klara and Cornelis Korteweg, it was that a full stomach, a warm bed, and routine made forgetting easy.

Now, in the kitchen with Mrs. Korteweg, she wondered if what her father had told her about German soldiers was also true about Dutch soldiers, about any soldier who joined the SS. Could Malka, or Maria, or however the real girl inside called herself, outsmart them all?

For eighteen months she had been living in Vught, protected by the Kortewegs, thanks to her father's connections in the underground and thanks, too, to her straight nose, blue eyes, and blonde hair. At the beginning, whenever the neighbors saw her in town buying sugar or new shoes and asked Mrs. Korteweg about the new girl living with them, Mrs. Korteweg said she was a distant cousin from the north of Holland whose parents had died suddenly. Over the months, everyone accepted that story. Even Malka grew to accept it, but now maybe Mrs. Korteweg wanted to upset the equilibrium. Why? Did she want to torture a Jew in her own way, in her own home, for killing her beloved Jesus?

"I want to meet him," Malka said, this time more forcefully.

"*Kom, kom hier,*" Mrs. Korteweg said. "We go meet the soldier." She took Malka by the hand. "Take off your net, Maria."

Malka took off the net. Her hair cascaded down her back and over her shoulders. Mrs. Korteweg touched the child's nose. As if to straighten it even more?

They walked into the parlor. He stopped playing, stood up, and saluted.

Malka forced herself not to laugh. Saluting Mrs. Korteweg? What kind of soldier was this?

"*Goeden middag*, Frans."

"*Goeden middag*, Mevrouw Korteweg."

"*Ja, ja*, this is Maria, my cousin's daughter. She comes to Vught from the north. Are you also from the north, Frans?"

"I am from Amsterdam."

Malka forced herself not to show any expression on her face.

"*Ja, ja*, well, Maria likes your playing very much."

The words sounded like a challenge to Malka, as if Klara Korteweg were saying, *OK, young man, now let's see if you can separate the true notes from the false, the cover from the hidden.*

"Maria. Maria," The soldier said her name twice, as if he were tasting a new pastry.

Malka lowered her head and blushed. The SS soldier walked over to her.

"My name is Frans," he said, his breath warming her face.

Malka froze. She hadn't been this close to a boy since she left Amsterdam and that was only Dovid, her third cousin, at a family bar mitzvah. Her hair was longer now. She wore a bra. Each night Mrs. Korteweg told her what a beautiful young Catholic girl she had become. Malka shielded her mouth with her hand.

"*Nee, nee*, don't hide, Maria," said the soldier. "Your lips are like wings."

Malka tried to keep breathing. She tried to remember the exact words her father had used at the train station, his blue woolen scarf wrapped around his neck, mist coming out of his mouth when he spoke. Were all soldiers stupid or just German soldiers?

She removed her hand and smiled and in that smile pushed down the last remnants of Malka Bienstock. Of course she was Maria and her lips were like wings of doves, wings of the Holy Spirit, Maria the good Catholic who kneeled and crossed and held the wafers between her lips and on her tongue and swallowed the wine and said her Hail Marys, "full of grace, the Lord is with thee," Maria Korteweg, the beautiful Catholic in Vught.

She looked at him. The young man's eyes held readiness like a delicate china cup. His dark-green uniform smelled of starch and sunshine. She tried to remember the color of her father's eyes but couldn't. Frans's blond hair fell gracefully onto his forehead, creating a fan above his eyebrows. Was her father's hair black or dark brown?

"I love Schubert," Maria said.

Frans invited Maria to sit on the leather chair that Cornelis occupied during the evenings. "This song I dedicate to you, Maria." He turned back to the piano, sat down on the bench, and, staring beyond the keys, lifted his fingers, as if he were about to touch the Holy Grail. His voice was like a bar mitzvah voice that had not yet changed.

Ave Maria! stainless styled!
Foul demons of the earth and air,
From this their wonted haunt exiled,
Shall flee before thy presence fair.

When he finished the song he looked at her. She hoped he didn't notice that everything inside her felt loose, as if all the parts of her life were unravelling like a sweater. She felt naked and scared.

He rose from the piano bench and handed her his handkerchief, which she was reluctant to take. It was white, starched, and perfectly clean. He insisted. She wiped her eyes and held the handkerchief over her mouth.

"Keep it, Maria," he said, his eyes boring into her with such intensity she didn't know which part of her body she wanted to cover first.

Maria sensed Mrs. Korteweg standing by the door, enjoying the first blush of romance.

"*Dank u*," Maria said. She stood up and bowed, curtsied, trying to copy some exit she had once seen in a movie in Amsterdam, taking a few steps backward toward the door with each ridiculous gesture, for Frans was no king or prince, merely a wounded SS soldier, yet she wanted to take leave slowly so that she would not crumble onto the floor in front of this new . . . this new angel who had appeared in her life, as if sent by God, coming with song.

At the end of the concert, the young Schwartzman stands up and takes a bow, without looking at the audience. Everyone claps as best they can. In the back row Malka stands up and holds on to the chair in front of her for support.

"Young man," she shouts over everyone's head, "can you play 'Ave Maria'?"

The retired Jews turn around. They give her a look as if she, Malka, has revealed the initial signs of Alzheimer's.

Yudit pulls on the elbow of Malka's linen jacket. "Sit down, Malki. Later we'll hear it."

"Look who's talking," Gershon calls out from the fifth row. Some of the people begin to snicker. "All *farputzt* for Holocaust Day."

"I should cry for not having been in Auschwitz?" Malka shouts back, feeling something has come undone. "Young man," she calls out, addressing the frail pianist, "play me a little 'Ave Maria.' *Bitte, bitte.*"

The young Schwartzman looks at Malka and then at his grandfather in the first row. He bows again, and when he straightens up, the director is marching to the front of the culture hall.

"Thank you for coming this morning," the director bellows, putting his heavy hand on the boy's plaid shoulder. "Everyone is now invited to the Blue Room to see the work of our own Mrs. Grossman, who photographed the first survivors coming off the boat at Haifa port in September 1945. Lunch is at twelve thirty, as usual." The director lifts his arms toward the aides, their sign to bring in the walkers and canes.

"*Lech l'azazel*," Malka shouts. "Go to hell. I want to hear 'Ave Maria.'" Malka is still standing, ignoring Yudit's efforts to get her to sit down. She pounds on the back of the plastic chair in front of her. "It is my right to make a request. This is still a free country. This is my Holocaust Day too."

The staff social worker, urged by the director's stiff finger in the air, glides over to Malka's seat and, standing behind her, rests her hands firmly on Malka's shoulders.

"Malka," she says, trying to maneuver her out of the culture hall, "Malka. It's all right. We know this is a difficult day. It's hard for all of us."

"Bullshit." Malka brushes away the social worker's arms and starts singing, "*Ave Maria, Jungfrau mild.*"

The social worker now grasps Malka's left wrist and pulls her out of the culture hall, while saying the event is over, the pianist gone.

"This is my Holocaust Day too," Malka says, almost shouting. "It is not my fault I was not in a camp. It is enough my parents died in one. This song is my memory and you can all go to hell."

Malka yanks her hand out of the social worker's grasp and stomps toward the elevator, singing "Ave Maria." Yudit shuffles behind her and enters the elevator just before the door shuts.

"Idiots," Malka says, pressing 2.

Yudit takes a breath and leans against the elevator wall. "In New York there was a man with a TV show," she says. "I think his name was Ed. It was the year we left. I don't know if he was Jewish. Maybe. He'd say, 'We have a really great shoe for you tonight.'" Yudit reaches out her hand to touch Malka's arm. "Malki, you gave us a really great shoe." Yudit lowers her hand to Malka's. "Now what in God's name is the matter?"

The two women get out on the second floor. Malka hands Yudit her key. "You open it."

Yudit opens the door for her friend. They walk into the small two-room suite and sit next to each other on the couch.

"So?" Yudit says.

"So! I can hardly remember my own father," Malka explodes, angry at the day. "I should remember six million?" She looks at the memory-recording machine on the coffee table, sitting next to her sewing scissors.

Yudit gets up, takes out a clean glass from the cupboard, and helps herself to a glass of water from the faucet. "Want one?" she asks, and prepares one for Malka without waiting for her reply.

"You want to hear the machine?" Malka says.

"What machine?"

"The audio cassette player. From the Memoir Lady."

"You play. I listen."

Malka has never had a friend like Yudit. She loves this woman, who she met when they were both sixty-six, both from Tel Aviv, both new at Beit Avraham, put there by their daughters, who wanted to make their own lives easier. As a teenager Malka had no close friends because she was in hiding. She had hoped her husband would become her best friend, but that didn't happen. Lily, her daughter, had been close, but ever since she moved Malka to "a good home in Jerusalem," as Lily calls Beit Avraham, their relationship has been strained. Yudit is her first true friend.

"It's long," Malka warns.

"I have where to go? At twelve thirty we eat."

The wall phone rings. Malka motions to Yudit to pick it up.

"Yes, she's fine now," Yudit says. "It's the day . . ."

"It's the Memoir Lady," Malka says after Yudit hangs up. "She asks me questions, probes, you know, like a lawyer. So now it all comes back in a stronger way."

"Front-row seat," says Yudit with her lovable smile. "With drinks! Don't cry, my dear. Here, take a tissue."

"It's my father," says Malka. "I miss him. You know what his last words were?"

"'Write!'"

"No. 'German soldiers are stupid.'" Malka takes a sip of water. "I couldn't remember anything, so she leaves me her machine and her felt-tip pen and tells me, 'Add anything you want on the tape or write.'"

"Who?"

"The Memoir Lady. This week, all of a sudden, I remember details. You sure you want to hear?"

"Do fish swim?" Yudit moves to the TV chair on the other side of the coffee table and puts her feet up on the matching leather stool. "Shoot."

Malka presses PLAY with her thumb.

I couldn't take my mind off this beautiful boy. Frans was his name. Even though he was wounded in his leg—I never asked how it happened. Maybe the Malka in me didn't want to know. I wanted to see him as if he had dropped from heaven, some angel who would save me and take me back to my family in Amsterdam. Even his uniform enticed me, the smell, the brass, the gold buttons. It was the uniform of the Grenadier Division Landstorm Nederland. Even though he was recovering from a wound—maybe his knee or ankle, I don't know—he still wore his uniform.

"Wait a minute, Malka. Turn off the machine. I have to go to the bathroom." Yudit gets up, goes, and then takes up a new position next to Malka on the couch.

"Ready?" asks Malka, her thumb on PLAY.

"Shoot."

Every Thursday afternoon he came over and every Thursday afternoon I sat and listened to him play. Each time he sang to me "Ave Maria." He looked straight at me when he sang. Not the keyboard. He knows the songs and the notes by heart. His voice is soft and high-pitched, like an angel's, as if he never grew up. Not a man's voice, but maybe I'm imagining. The song stayed with me throughout the week until he came again the next Thursday. While he practiced at the Kortewegs' I always had what to look forward to. My whole week revolved around his practicing and singing to me on

Thursdays. Mrs. Korteweg let me sit in the parlor with him and listen up close. Maybe she thought I would fall in love and convert and stay in Vught after the war. Maybe she wanted him to catch me. I don't know what moved her. All I know is I was falling for this young man in the SS.

Then one day he tells me he is being sent back to his unit on the front. Which front? I wonder, but I don't say anything. I was miserable. I wanted to leave too. But I had nowhere to go. The woman from the underground had stopped contacting me. I had food, clothes, even my own room, but there was no life there, except for those Thursday afternoons. I missed my parents, my brother and friends in Amsterdam. I hadn't seen them for two years. I had no idea what had become of anyone. The Kortewegs had a radio in their bedroom. Sometimes we listened to broadcasts in the evening, but they did not want me to listen too much. We never spoke of Jews.

On his last day he asked . . .

"Who?" says Yudit. Malka hits STOP.

"Frans."

"The husband?"

"No, the soldier."

"Ahh, the Nazi . . ."

. . . if I would walk him through the forest back to his convalescent home. I was ecstatic. I had never been outside the house with him, alone. Mrs. Korteweg didn't seem to mind, so I went with him. There was a gate between the Kortewegs' land and the forest and by the gate a linden tree. He took a knife out of his pocket and carved our names in the tree, just like in the song.

"Which song?" Yudit asks. Malka hits STOP.

"'Der Lindenbaum.'"

"Ahh, yah yah. I remember now."

Then he held my hand and we walked into the forest. His hand was almost twice as large as mine and soft like the paraffin before it cools. My hand felt so good nestled in his. I wanted his fingers to touch me all over. I wanted to be his piano. We walked in silence on the dirt path that led from the Korteweg house to his convalescent home. The last rays of sunlight pierced the branches of pines and oaks. Time stopped. I wanted to walk to Portugal with Frans and get on a ship and leave Europe forever.

"You could have come to Brooklyn," Yudit says.

Birds chirped. A magic hour . . . I . . . with my soldier . . .

"The Nazi . . ."

I wanted to run away . . . with . . . He must have felt my growing love or longing or whatever it was.

"Confusion," pipes Yudit.

He stopped and turned toward me. He wove his long fingers through my hair. Holding my head, he kissed me on the lips. I closed my eyes and let him. I felt empty and full at the same time. I leaned into him so hard I felt his ribs . . .

"That's not the only thing . . ."

. . . through his uniform. Slowly I moved my arms up to his shoulders and put them around his neck. With his tongue he opened my mouth as if opening a letter and then he forced his tongue into my mouth and explored it . . . like a cave . . . shining a light inside me.

"Can I have more water?"

Malka presses STOP, gets up, and fills Yudit's glass. "Do you want to hear the rest?"

"Sure. I'm just thirsty."

"Ready?" Malka says when Yudit sits down next to her again.

"Shoot," says Yudit.

The bar mitzvah boys in Amsterdam never did anything like

that. This was my first kiss. I loved Frans. All the branches of all the trees in the forest celebrated that kiss.

I had put on some lipstick for this occasion, stolen it from Mrs. Korteweg's top drawer, to be exact.

"Dark, like today's?"

After the kiss I licked his neck and by accident got some lipstick on the shirt collar of his uniform.

"Verboden," Yudit says. "Strikt verboden."

I didn't say anything and of course he couldn't see it, but I knew he might get in trouble when he returned to his convalescent home. Maybe they would demote him. I didn't know. What did I know? I was young and cut off from the world.

"So that was the end of Hitler?"

"Frans."

He told me I shouldn't walk with him any farther because it was getting dark. He told me after the war he would come back for me and take me home to meet his parents. Instead of looking in his eyes, I stared at the smudge on his collar. I kissed him again on the lips. Then he sent me back to the Kortewegs. I turned and ran through the forest. It was totally dark outside when I reached the house. I ran to my room and threw myself on the bed and cried. I knew I would never see him again and I knew I was no longer a Jew in hiding. I was just a brokenhearted silly girl who loved an SS soldier.

"It's OK. We have another twenty minutes till lunch."

Vught was liberated from the German occupation before the winter of '44, but I stayed with the Kortewegs until the war ended. They were decent people and took a huge risk to keep me in their home. After the summer of '45, when it was all over, they wanted me to convert to Catholicism and stay. I waited for my parents, but as stories about the Dutch Jews started circulating, I wanted to go back to Amsterdam to see for myself. One day they put me on a train and off I went. Only in the coming days ... months ... years did I begin to comprehend the disaster. Every time I thought about my mother, father, and brother, I thought of Frans in the forest. I imagined our kiss took place as my parents entered the gas chamber. I've never ... is this enough, Edith?

"So did he come looking, this soldier?"

"I never saw him again. When I contacted the Kortewegs in '48, before I left Holland, they said he had come once asking for me, but they told him they didn't know where I was."

"And he believed them?"

"Maybe my father was right . . ." Malka gets up and walks to her dresser. From the top drawer she takes out a white handkerchief. When she sits back down on the couch, she blows her nose. Yudit puts an arm around her.

"It's all in the past, Malki. Over and done . . ."

Malka sits in silence.

"No. It's not done," she says in a soft voice. "I still feel guilty. My family was dead, but I pined for Frans. I remember that kiss as if it happened this morning."

"We should be so lucky . . ." Yudit says. "Who doesn't remember their first kiss? We all do, Malki, even if we can't remember the chap's name."

Malka gets up and goes into the bathroom. When she comes out, her lips are aflame with renewed Root Red.

"We're not guilty," Yudit says. "It wasn't our fault. Let's stop torturing ourselves." She looks at her watch. "It's time for lunch."

"I hate this day," Malka says, as she walks over to the memory machine and presses EJECT with her thumb. The tape flips out. Malka takes it in her left hand and with her right grabs her sewing scissors on the table and cuts the tape and then pulls it off the reel and cuts more, pulls and cuts, pulls and cuts, all the time saying, "I hate this life."

Yudit stands up and raises her voice. "Malka, Malki, what are you doing? That's *your* life. Don't destroy it." She tries to take the scissors away from Malka, but Malka pushes her arm away and keeps cutting until the pieces of the magnetic tape are strewn across the coffee table and the floor, like pieces of debris blown in from a strange wind.

Malka collapses onto the couch. "Not the one I wanted," she says, her hands covering her face.

Yudit sits down next to Malka and puts her arm around her shoulders. "Did anybody ask us?" she says, taking a tissue out of her pocket. After a few moments of silence Yudit says, "Hail Mary, full of lace," and the two friends chuckle. They decide to get all *farputzt* again for lunch, this time with powder, rouge, eye shadow, the works.

Waiting for the elevator, Malka tells Yudit that Edith gave her empty tapes. "Maybe I'll make another one." For the first time since this morning, she feels lighter.

"You can change the ending," Yudit says.

"Right," Malka says, as if Yudit has opened a door. "I can say whatever I want. The Memoir Lady doesn't give a shit, as long as it's fifty pages. Anyway, it's not for her, or even for the grandchildren. It's for me. It's *my* story. I'm going to tell about the *real* horror, the one *after* the war when we went back home and everyone was gone. Gone."

The elevator comes and Malka continues, as if a new road has appeared in her past, "I will describe the malicious silence that filled the hallways. In every house good people had given our names to the SS. They continued to eat their breakfast with their delicate cups and plum jams, but they welcomed us back with shock in their eyes. *What? We did not rid ourselves of all of our Jews?*"

Yudit listened with love.

"That is the story I will tell, not some childish flirtation with a stupid Dutch boy. And I will leave two blank black pages in the center of the book to commemorate those days and months *after* the war, when there was no light, no hope, and no family. Let our grandchildren learn to read that darkness, the wail beyond words."

Yudit takes Malka's hand and kisses it. "Hail Mary," she says. "Another great shoe."

The elevator opens and the two survivors march into the dining room. "*Yallah*," says Yudit, "let us now concentrate on guessing the ingredients in today's Holocaust stew."

"Hail Mary," shouts Malka so everyone can hear, and they hug each other right there in the middle of the dining room.

Herzl the Vegetable Guy

All the kids on the Castel laughed at me 'cause my name was Herzl. They said the founder of the state can't even read. I hit them and the principal kicked me out of fourth grade, so my father came. He had a stall in Mahaneh Yehuda and was well respected. After he turned over the principal's desk, the principal let me back in. I wasn't bad in math, so when my uncle opened this place, I helped him after school. I was good at arranging the fruit too, so when my uncle goes to pray mincha, I run the shop.

Once an old lady from across the street comes in and asks my name and I tell her Herzl. She thinks I'm making fun of her, so I charge her double for the oranges, but she never told my uncle. A cousin wants to open a stall on the other side of Bethlehem Road. This makes us very mad, taking over our turf. There aren't enough streets in Jerusalem? Let him open on Palmach. Tonight we're meeting at home to settle the matter. After my mother's kubbeh soup, everything works out.

Thank you to all my customers. I love serving you and will continue to do so for decades. As one of you taught me: There are two Herzls. One sold a cockamamie dream and the other sells onions!

DISPERSION, A TALE

T he Queen knew she and the King needed some R & R at Solomon's in Eilat if the marriage was to survive. They hadn't talked to each other, soul talk, for three years. Not because they didn't have what to say, but because, between his trucking and her mothering, the effort to anoint thirty minutes for themselves resembled that needed to climb Mount Sinai in Tamuz. Who had the energy?

One Thursday night, during halftime of a Tel Aviv basketball game when Maccabi was leading by twelve points, the Queen finagled the King's agreement to a desert jaunt. Just the two of them.

"OK, OK," the King gasped, hoping she'd back off before game time. "We'll go. We'll go. I'll take care of everything."

"Everything" meant finding a solution for their seven sons and Dina.

The Queen bragged about her upcoming vacation to the women at the well. "Gee," they hummed in unison. "I wish my king would take me to Eilat."

After Maccabi lost by only two stinking points, the King felt he had lost everything. Not only his bets, but also three days' vacation to the Queen. His luck changed at the Sonol Station on Bethlehem Road.

There were people going back and forth in the Land in those days. Suissa was one of them. An impeccably dressed fellow, Suissa sold cattle sperm in Cairo—the only Israeli product (if you can put a nationality on sperm) the Egyptians were buying three years after the peace treaty. Suissa and the King were filling up their tanks at the same island. The King overheard Suissa tell the gas station attendant about a family he knew in Cairo with eight kids. The King's wheels started rolling and two minutes later he asked Suissa if he would take the King's eight children to visit this family in Cairo.

"Are they good travelers?" Suissa shouted, as he handed the attendant his gold Visa card.

"No problema," the King shouted back. "The firstborn will roughhouse with his younger brothers in the back seat of your van and the daughter will sketch Mount Sinai with felt-tip pens. They also know gematria travel games."

"OK," said Suissa, "it's a deal. I take the eight kids for three days and"—Suissa took out a calculator from an inside pocket of his suit and pushed some buttons—"you pay me 3,000 shekels. That's 375 shekels a kid, including gas, food, lodging, the works."

"Who is this joker?" the Queen asked in a raised voice that evening when the King told her about the arrangement. "Some smooth-talking guy you picked up at a garage?"

"Gas station."

"That means he's reliable, right? I hope you told him to take the long route, so the kids can see the old stomping ground."

The King hated it when the Queen brought up their past. Why couldn't she forget? The present was hard enough, with inflation up 400 percent and people looking for work in other countries.

"Will they be safe?" the Queen asked.

"Sure, they'll be safe," the King lied. "Suissa has eight seatbelts in his van."

Soon all the progeny were hanging around the kitchen, waiting for dinner. Their parents told them about their upcoming journey.

"Not Egypt again!" cried Avihud.

The King closed in on the fridge to see what he could nosh before dinner.

"I don't want to go back to Egypt," said Dina.

Then the firstborn, Aviel, the most troublesome of the eight, began. "Remember what happened last time we were there?" His eyes gleamed with sadistic delight as he slunk in front of his father, opened the fridge door, and reached for the leftover tuna. "Remember, Pops?"

The King's hunger was now mingled with anger, a dangerous combination. He tried to calm himself by swallowing, lest he strike his firstborn in the ribs. Not that he'd succeed, since the kid was stronger than he was. Still, the King thought to himself, a King is a King. He pressed his hands into his son's shoulders, but the son slithered away. "Remember, Pops?" he taunted.

The Queen smelled an explosive situation. She enlisted her calm voice. "Now let's stop all this fuss. Your father and I are going to Eilat for three days. You're all going to Egypt. Everything will be fine, just like it always is."

Dina piped up, "Why do you have to be alone with Abba for three days and two nights?" She ran to hug her father, but Aviel tripped her with his left foot.

"Yeah," the brothers added, like a chorus. "What do you have in Eilat that you don't have here?"

The King sat down at the table and waited to be served. "Pack lightly," he said authoritatively. "It's Av."

Aviel laughed as he sat down next to his father. "You know what that means, Pops." He dipped his forefinger into the tuna and licked it with gusto.

"No, what does it mean, son?"

"Means we gotta be back here in Jerusalem by the Ninth, so we can wail."

The Queen interjected, "OK, dear, it's a deal. You go with Suissa for three days and we promise you'll be back by the Ninth to mourn."

The King gave the Queen a dirty look, but remained silent. He knew if they started bartering the Ninth, then the firstborn, whose memory was sharp as a dagger, would bring up the Tenth, the Seventeenth, and all the other traumatic landmarks along their shared history. A boy this gifted was bothersome to have around. He never let his parents forget anything. The last thing the King wanted right now, before dinner, was to be reminded of that night long ago when the King nearly killed his son.

The Queen talked about it all the time with the women at the well. Each time she repeated the story, she added a detail or embellished the critical moment. It became their favorite story.

We went for a picnic on Mount Moriah with two other families.

It got dark. We found wood and logs, so we made a fire. One family brought hot dogs.

Kosher? one woman always asked.

We sat around eating and singing, but the eldest couldn't keep his hands away from the fire, as if he were tempting the flames to burn him. Every time the King said, "No," the kid said, "Yes." Every time I said, "Sit," the kid stood. Our friends' children cuddled with their parents, sang campfire songs, and ate hot dogs. Only our son made trouble.

Then what happened? the women at the well always asked.

Suddenly, a donkey wandered by and the kid started chasing it. He wanted to play giddyup. "No sir," I told him, and I gave the little monster a swat on his behind. He cried. I swatted him again. Why couldn't he be like all the other good little boys and girls?

Then what happened? the women at the well asked.

The kid started shaking and running toward the fire, as if he wanted to jump in head-first. The King leaped forward. He lurched at the kid from behind. He pulled him down onto our picnic blanket, just as the firstborn's head hung over a blue flame.

"Are you crazy?" he shouted in his face. Then he started beating the kid with both hands.

"Stop, stop," the firstborn cried.

"I can't, I can't," the King replied.

"You're hurting me," the firstborn cried.

"You hurt me, you little monster," the King replied.

The women sat rapt. They forgot to pull up their jugs from the well. *What happened next?* they asked.

Suddenly, the earth opened and out jumped a . . . a . . .

Nu? What jumped out? the women begged.

A cat! Out jumped a cat from the bowels of the earth and leaped onto the enmeshed father and son and bit the father's hand.

Was it black, the cat? asked a woman who obeyed all the commandments.

That's not the point, said another. *The point is the cat saved the son.*

That's one interpretation, the Queen said. *Some say the person saved was the King. And some say what jumped out of the earth wasn't a cat, but a she-devil. And others said they saw a large hand come out of the fire and wrench the King away from his son. You see, ladies, it was dark, the only light coming from the campfire. Nobody knew exactly what happened, because nobody saw the whole picture. Anyway, that was the end of the picnic.*

The women drew up their heavy jugs of water. They all agreed that only Hieronymus Bosch could paint such a scene.

On the day of their departure, the King and Queen awoke at six. While the King was outside packing the tent, bathing suits, towels, and seven tins of sardines into the trunk of their used Subaru, the Queen dished out eight bowls of Rice Krispies and sliced eight bananas. Then she planted goodbye kisses on the backs of eight stiff necks. The King came in and said, "Now be good little children and don't get into mischief. Suissa will be here at seven thirty."

When the King and Queen reached Sodom, the Queen started feeling guilty.

"I know we need quiet time together, to figure out who we are and why we stay together," she told the King who was driving and puffing, "but maybe we could have found a simpler arrangement for the next generation, one that didn't entail so much wandering."

The King ignored her. He drove and puffed, drove and puffed.

"This Suissa fellow . . ." she continued.

"Yeah?"

"What impressed you about him?"

"His tie. The fact that he wore a tie in Tamuz," he said.

The couple sat in silence as the King raced by the Dead Sea Works at 130 kilometers an hour.

"No. Not just his tie," the King continued. "He wore a tie clip too, and not just any tie clip." The King pushed down harder on the gas and puffed smoke in the Queen's face. "I need silence now," said the King.

"Suissa could sell a parking lot to a shepherd," said the Queen, as they passed a mirage.

Three hours later, a row of date palms interspersed with pink oleander welcomed the King and Queen to Eilat in the name of the municipality. A wide sky swept down to cradle the amber mountains, white sand, and turquoise water.

Breathe deeply, the Queen told herself. *Take in the Land.*

Overcome by the unusual beauty of the place, the King extinguished his cigarette. How meaningless to mention borders in this garden. Nonetheless, the King and Queen parked at Solomon's near Taba. They set up their green and yellow camping tent in twelve minutes, next to a Danish couple with a four-year-old girl who ran naked in and out of the water, shouting "Mommy, Mommy, look at me." The King and Queen lay down in the tent's shade, facing the lapping water.

"Let's open up," the Queen used as an opener.

"OK," the King said. "You first."

Gradually, like turtles, the King and Queen started to talk, one's speech flowing toward the other on shimmering heatwaves.

With great determination, for they both wanted the family to survive, they did Expectations, Food, Land, Garbage, and Money, the way the Danish couple made love—day and night. The King and Queen ate sardines as they reviewed that frightening episode on Mount Moriah when the King nearly killed their firstborn. For years they hadn't discussed the incident. If the Queen brought it up, the King would immediately fall asleep. But now he stayed awake, and it dominated their R & R in Eilat. They argued about whose fault it was.

"You were too passive," the Queen reproved the King.

"No. You were too active," the King countered.

Each blamed the other for setting no limits.

"We get lost without boundaries," the Queen mused. "I have trouble with borders."

"Yeah," the King added. "It's complicated. But still . . ."

By the second night, even though each had a different version of what exactly happened and even *when* it happened, both agreed that the incident released them from fears of their own destructiveness.

"We'll never kill our children," the Queen summarized, and gave the King a hug.

"Yeah," he responded and hugged back.

The Queen ran her fingers through the King's hairy chest. "We have discovered evil, ambivalence, and unity. Let's go home."

The King lit a cigarette. "Now I'm ready for more," he said, stroking the Queen's sandy hair with his free hand.

"More what?" asked the Queen.

"More . . . whatever it's called."

Early in the morning on the third day, the King and Queen packed their tent into the car. "Tell your parents goodbye," the Queen called to the little Dane making sandcastles and moats.

There was more traffic now, as pilgrims filed to Jerusalem by foot, car, camel, and bus to commemorate the Ninth of Av. The Queen noticed that some of the pilgrims started weeping while still in the Arava. She marveled at the strength of religious fervor.

By the rivers of Babylon,
There we sat down and wept
As we remembered Zion.

The Queen sang in a disco beat and clapped her hands.

"You're not supposed to clap," the King reminded her.

The apartment was empty when the King and Queen arrived home. Eight cereal bowls were stacked on the table, milk in the top one yellow. An ominous calm hovered around the fridge. Just as the Queen was throwing their damp towels into the washing machine, Suissa entered with the children.

The King and the Queen rushed to greet them.

"How was it?" they blurted together.

"Not bad," the more responsive ones replied, taking their places at the table.

"What's to eat?" asked Avidan.

The Queen counted heads and got to seven.

"Where's the firstborn?" she asked Suissa.

"I sold him in Cairo," Suissa replied nonchalantly, helping himself to a peach rotting in the fruit bowl. "Got a pretty good price," he said, taking a bite.

"What do you mean you sold him in Cairo?" the Queen

shrieked. "We didn't hire you to sell our children." She handed him a napkin. "Now I want you to get your ass right back down there and bring him home. He has his first physical next week."

"I'm afraid I can't do that. The Egyptians took such a liking to your son—clever kid you've got there—that they grabbed him for the royal court. He's tutoring seventh graders in computer science." Suissa threw the naked pit into the sink.

"What does he know about computers?" the King bellowed. "All he does is watch television."

"Well, the Egyptians found him exceptionally talented, and nice looking, I may add. They may even send him to their Polyanalytic Institute."

"What the hell is that?" the King demanded.

"Oh, I don't know. Some place along the Nile where they study dreams."

"What kind of bullshit is this?" The Queen looked toward heaven, but saw only the mold from last year's rain. "I entrust my children to a traveling salesman for three stinking days and he sells the eldest to the Egyptians?" Now she approached Suissa and saw his tie clip. "What do you think he is? Cattle sperm?"

"Let's call the police," the King said.

"Oh, I'm afraid that would be a waste of time, Sir," Suissa said. "You see, my brother is the Chief of Police. We Suissas always stick together." His seedy eyes roamed the room for another snack.

The children showed their parents the turquoise scarab pins that their new Egyptian friends had bought them in the Cairo market. Both King and Queen found them creepy. "How nice," they said.

The King wondered if the children were in cahoots with Suissa, since they expressed no regret at their brother's absence.

"I think the kids like Suissa a little too much," the King whispered to the Queen. "What's in those scarab pins?"

"I think you're right," the Queen replied. "I smell a rat."

Suissa hung around for another forty minutes, expecting remuneration. The King and Queen made it perfectly clear not one shekel would be exchanged until all eight children were back home at 63 Bethlehem Road where they belonged.

Suissa finally stomped out of the apartment, cursing the utopian Ingathering of the Exiles.

"Can we go to the Wall now and wail?" the children asked.

Without the firstborn around, sibling rivalry dropped below sea level. The date of the first physical passed, as did the induction, swearing-in ceremony, Chanukah, Purim, and Pesach, without a word from the firstborn. Not even a blintz on Shavuot. The King adjusted quickly to the new situation, but the Queen was broken.

"I am faint and exceedingly crushed," the Queen told the King one night.

"What do you mean?"

"No sooner do we patch up our relationship than our family breaks down. My heart goes around in circles as I make myself crazy trying to figure out what we did wrong. My strength has left me."

"You read too many psalms," the King told her.

Then the Queen got a brilliant idea. "Why don't you go down to Egypt and bring him back! He could still make it by the Ninth."

The King needed some convincing, but by the end of the evening news, he knew what he had to do. At six the next morning he was on the 405 direct to Tel Aviv. There, he caught an air-conditioned tourist bus to Cairo.

The Queen sat home in the afternoon and watched *The Ten Commandments* with her daughter. "Stop crying," the daughter told her mother. "It's only a story."

Meanwhile, in Egypt, the King sneaked into the royal court. Hiding behind a potted date palm, he spotted his firstborn, who now sported a punk haircut and was teaching DOS to seventh graders. With drama, the King revealed himself to his son.

"It's me, your father."

The son called his guard. "Who is this intruder?"

"It's me, son. The King. Don't you remember? The guy who used to take you to the zoo. Remember? We'd feed the monkeys chewing gum when the guards weren't looking."

"Guard, arrest this man," the son ordered in Arabic and returned to the ERASE command.

"But it's me, sonny boy. King. Pops, to you. I love you, kid. Honest I do. And your *ema* misses you. We didn't mean to kill you that day on Mount Moriah. Honest."

The bodyguard grabbed the King from behind.

"We were just playing, kid. Having a good time. Remember the campfire? And the songs? You know, the way families do."

When the King started yelling about the picnic, the bodyguard dragged him away. "You gotta remember, son. You remember everything. Don't bullshit me." Now he was kicking his legs, and the potted date palm fell. "You'll see when you have little ones of your own, you son of a bitch. You'll see what it's like with fathers and sons."

"Take him away, I tell you," the punk computer specialist shouted.

~⊙~

The bodyguard threw the intruder into the royal prison. A thin guard approached and gave the troublemaker a cup of spoiled garbanzo beans. A fat guard came and gave the troublemaker a dirty glass of water. The King lay down on a straw mat and fell asleep, hungry and thirsty.

The firstborn came to his father in a dream, dressed like a cat with ram's horns. *I really do recognize you,* the cat-ram said in the dream. *I just don't want my seventh graders to know who I am.* Then he poked his horns into his father's side. *How are Ema and Sis?* He didn't ask about his brothers. *How's Tel Aviv Maccabi doing, Pops?*

The cat-ram explained that he now spoke perfect Egyptian Arabic. Since he was the top student at the dream institute, he had been chosen to interpret the future for the kings of Egypt. This promised him job security, since there would always be a future.

The King tried to talk to the cat-ram, but no words came out of his mouth. He hoped the animal could read his silence, but apparently the kid was more adept at interpreting dreams than silence.

The King pointed to the east, then made a pillow motion with his hands and pretended he was snoring. He hoped the cat-ram would understand that he was telling him to return home with him. Maybe he did, because the creature continued to rave about Egypt—the food, the women, the Nile. *I got a great barber,* the cat-ram added for emphasis.

The King cried out, but his son could not hear.

I have no need for your cursed land, the cat-ram yelled. Then the animal threw the King a white muslin drawstring bag full of fifty gold coins.

Take this money, he said, and leave me alone.

The King picked up the bag.

Wait until the next drought, the King said, raising his hands toward heaven. Then we'll see how much the Egyptians value you.

Prophecy! All I get from you is depressing prophecy, the cat-ram yelled, as he climbed out of the dream.

It was exactly at this point that the King awoke in a panic and kicked the cup of garbanzo beans onto the cold stone floor.

"Guard, guard," he shouted. That his voice was loud and robust did not escape his amazement. "Let me out of here, you jerks. Here, take this. Fifty gold coins. Open the lock. I promise to be on the first bus back to Tel Aviv.

Now it just so happened that the fat guard had to pay his son's high-school registration fee the next day and didn't have enough cash, so it didn't take much bribery to convince him to pick up the muslin bag. While the thin guard was still asleep, the fat guard unlocked the gate. The King ran all the way to the closest bus station, leaving a trail of squished garbanzo beans behind. He caught an overcrowded, smelly bus to El Arish.

Arriving at the central bus station in Tel Aviv twenty hours later, the King fell off the bus and kissed the asphalt pavement.

When he walked into his home, the Queen was watching a condensed version of the Academy Awards, along with four billion other viewers outside the continental United States. Before she could learn who won the best script of the year, she turned off the TV and listened to her husband's rendition of what happened in Egypt.

"I am faint and exceedingly crushed," she wailed, after the King finished.

The route from pain to prayer, my dear friends, is a short one. It takes the Queen only five minutes by bus to go from Bethlehem Road to Rachel's Tomb. That's the little round one across the street from Ahmed's garage, a short walk from the Church of the Nativity. The Queen goes there every morning to pray. Inside the tomb, she moves her chapped lips frenetically against the cold stone wall, pleading to God for the return of her firstborn, if not for a Friday night dinner, then at least for the next Ninth of Av.

Her girlfriends from the well join her in the tomb from time to time to pray for their own sons, all of whom are entrenched in their own little Egypts, this one selling plastics in Vegas, that one practicing law in Boca. Sometimes, when the women return together to Jerusalem on the bus, they beg the Queen to tell them their favorite story, the one about the fire and the kid, the one that takes place on that crazy mountain, the one that keeps happening a long, long time ago.

DISCUSSION QUESTIONS
FOR BOOK CLUBS,
WRITING GROUPS, AND
INDIVIDUAL READERS

---

1. INGATHERING OF AN EXILE

In this story, John, who becomes Yonatan, sees Hebrew letters on the branches of trees, on falling leaves, and on the palms of his hands. What do you think happens to immigrants when they learn a new language? Is a language just words? What are the options for how the mother tongue and the acquired language live in one body?

2. SIMON, THE TALE OF AN ASPIRING JEW

Often young people in their early twenties suddenly change and adopt a new way of life. What is gained and what is lost in such a dramatic shift? What are alternative courses for spiritual enlightenment?

3. ANNIE AND TED

How does hero worship affect one's development? Are heroes necessary? Why? Who are your heroes and what influence do they play in your life?

4. LAW OF RETURN

Laura had no idea what she was getting into when she purchased an apartment on Bethlehem Road. Has the history of your house or apartment ever cast a spell over you? How does your city's history affect your everyday life? What kind of commitment do we have to those who came before us?

5. WEDDING DRESS

How does a piece of clothing speak to your deepest needs, like the wedding dress spoke to Efrat? Give examples and share your stories of a particular piece of clothing. Write a story in which this piece of clothing becomes a character.

6. THE FIRST PREGNANCY IN JERUSALEM

Helen went a little crazy during her first pregnancy. How does place affect your well-being—the names of streets, towns, states, specific geography—before pregnancy, during, and afterward? How does a specific pregnancy affect the parents' initial attitudes toward the newborn?

7. EVERY MAN A LAMB

Often, our inner lives become visible during extreme situations. For Dr. Coen, the episode of a ritual slaughter brought out his inner aggression. Think of examples in your own life when your own behavior surprised or scared you. Share with the group.

8. GET OUT OF JAIL

A parent's absence in the family, especially for a hospitalization, can cause imbalance in the family dynamics when the parent returns. Sometimes the return is for the better and sometimes it is for the worse. Did you experience such crises when you were a child? What does Pat's clinging to her purse and its contents say about her relationship with her mother?

9. HOMECOMING, 1982

Many soldiers bring their wartime experiences home with them, like Les. If disturbing behavior continues for months, the person is said to be suffering from post-traumatic stress disorder and needs professional care. Only in the past decades have modern armies learned to deal with this aspect of war in a way that can help families survive. How do you think war causes the behavior that Les exhibits? How could his wife have helped him?

10. INVENTORY

Leaving a beloved place is often difficult. Nechama overcomes her fear by naming the items she wants to take with her. Do you think creating such an inventory helps? If so, how? If not, why? Create your own inventory of a room and see which objects speak to you, which objects shed light on special memories.

11. MALKA'S HOLOCAUST

Malka cannot accept a certain part of her life, and she is angry at society's belittling her survival after the Holocaust. What can she do with her guilt? Who profits most from remembrance days? Are such days important and, if so, why?

12. DISPERSION, A TALE

Every leaving is an arrival, until the next leaving. Bigger words for this process are *immigration* and *exile*. The Jewish people have gone through this cycle for millennia. How does this cycle play out in the individual family? How do the stories we read over and over again, like the Binding of Isaac, play out in our own family life, if at all?

ACKNOWLEDGMENTS

Over decades, many talented and generous people have helped me nurse and nudge these stories into shape. I am grateful to each one. First, the editors who published some of the stories: Guest editor Marilyn Hacker at *The Kenyon Review* in summer 1993 published "Dispersion, A Tale"; former editors Alan M. Tigay and Zelda Shluker at *Hadassah Magazine* published "Explosion," a shorter version of "The Ingathering of an Exile" in June/July 2007; Nora Gold published "Every Man a Lamb" on Jewishfiction.net in February 2011 and "Inventory" in September 2025; Gabrielle David, editor-in-chief at *phati'tude Literary Magazine* published "Law of Return" in fall 2011; Catherine Parnell at *Consequence: An International Literary Magazine Focusing on the Culture of War* published "Homecoming, 1982" in spring 2018; Elissa Wald and David Michael Slater at Judithmagazine.substack.com published "Malka's Holocaust" in September 2025.

A huge thank-you to Joan Leegant and Amital Stern, who each offered invaluable encouragement, suggestions, and guidance over the many years of writing these stories. Both writers are models of generosity. Emma Lawson, an extremely conscientious copy editor, made the process enjoyable. Thank you to Susan Kennedy for her close reading.

These stories are far better than their first drafts, due to the mentoring of Professor Allen Hoffman from the Shaindy Rudoff Graduate Program in Creative Writing at Bar-Ilan University. I am grateful to him for his incessant urging to "get them out into the world." Others who have helped me understand the stories better are Peter Stine, Chris Noel, Evan Fallenberg, Nat Sobel, and Julie Stevenson.

The team at She Writes Press has given me not only a valuable publishing experience but also a warm community. Kudos to Brooke Warner for creating a caring home for women writers.

I am grateful for my partner, David Kurz, who has been supportive of my writing life since 2005.

Without my three children, that is, my three miracles, I never would have become a mother. Thank you to their father and to them for grounding me on Bethlehem Road for so many wonderful and challenging years.

ABOUT THE AUTHOR

photo credit: Debbi Cooper

JUDY LEV is an American Israeli writer living in Israel since 1967. For decades she wrote a personal essay column in *The Jerusalem Post* and *The Cleveland Jewish News* under the name Judy Labensohn. She has worked as a certified social worker with bereaved families and as a tour guide at Neot Kedumim, The Biblical Landscape Reserve in Israel. Lev has been a pioneer of teaching creative writing in English in Israel.

Our Names Do Not Appear, her first book, which takes place in Cleveland and Jerusalem, is a memoir of silenced childhood grief. Her stories and essays have appeared in *The Kenyon Review, Michigan Quarterly Review, Southwest Review, Creative Nonfiction, Fourth Genre, Hadassah Magazine,* and *Lilith,* among others, and several anthologies and college texts, such as *Other Words: A Writer's Reader,* from UMass Amherst Writing Program. She was a Pushcart Prize nominee in 2013. Since October 2024, she has been writing "Epistles from Israel" on Substack.

A mother of three and grandmother of five, Lev holds two graduate writing degrees, one in creative nonfiction from Goucher College and one in fiction from Bar-Ilan University.

She enjoys music, cutting hair and dancing, though not at the same time.

www.judylev.com
Judylabensohn.substack.com

Looking for your next great read?

We can help!

Visit www.shewritespress.com/next-read
or scan the QR code below for a list
of our recommended titles.

She Writes Press is an award-winning
independent publishing company founded to
serve women writers everywhere.